KNOCKED DOWN BY LOVE AND PICKED UP BY A DOPE BOY 2

NIDDA

Visit Our Website To Sign-up For Our Mailing List
www.UrbanChaptersPublications.com
If you would like to join our team, submit the first 3-4 chapters of your completed manuscript to
Submissions@UrbanChapterspublications.com

Be sure to join our reading group to connect with all authors under Urban Chapters Publications.
www.facebook.com/chillin'with UCP
Text Jahquel to 345345!
Be sure to bless our page with a LIKE!

This book is dedicated to Jeanette Breedlove. I could write a book about all the memories that I have with you. The love that you showed me since I met you is like nothing that I ever experienced. You treated me like blood, from day one. Me and lulu would be mad at each other and I was still at your house lol.

I wish I could come to your house right now and play cards. I never had a dull moment when I was at your home. It was always a party and you never put me like you did everybody else. Lol. The love that you showed everybody that was in your presence was one of a kind. You will be truly be missed forever! Rest peacefully.

1

AHMINA

"What the fuck are you doing answering my door?" Ace spat as he appeared in the doorway.

"You're not my dad, Aiden," the bitch replied as the lil boy waved at me while they disappeared into the house.

Looking up at Ace, I just knew that I would be overjoyed when I saw him and he would feel the same. I can't even describe the feeling that I'm have right now. The mug on his face, I can't help but be confused; he's supposed to be happy to see me. Looking back at Mo searching for answers, she was muggin' Ace too, really confusing me.

Looking down at Tiana sleep in my arms, not wanting to wake her up, I struggled to stay calm. Being confined to this damn wheelchair was also restricting me from acting the way that I wanted to. The pain in my chest felt like my heart was physically breaking and neither one of us said anything. Fighting back the tears that were burning the back of my eyes, I tried to wrap my head around what the fuck was going on.

"Who the fuck is she?" I asked, stopping Ace as he went to touch me.

"Who the fuck is who?" Ace questioned with an attitude.

"Nigga, I'm the one that just got out of a coma. The bitch that just answered the door. Now you got amnesia?" I questioned, feeling my pain turning into anger.

"Watch yo' fuckin' mouth when you talkin' to me," Ace demanded, swiftly turning my wheelchair around and lifting my chair over the threshold.

"Answer my question," I replied, changing my tone.

"Mina, this is my sister, Dani. Dani, this is Mina. Zay, this is TT Mina," Ace said as I turned back around and the bitch and the baby were standing in front of me.

"Annie said she not my TT," Zay replied and ran away.

Instead of pushing me through the house, Ace just stood behind me doing somethin'. Me and Dani just stared at each other in silence, not even speaking. I don't think that Ace would lie to me about having a sister. I damn sure don't remember him ever telling me that he had one. Which caused me to turn around and see why he hadn't started pushing me through the house. Ace was standing in front of the door stopping Mo from coming in the house. What the fuck is going on between them? Ace never fucked with Mo like that, but what the fuck could have happened? Why are they acting like this with each other?

"What is wrong with y'all? Ace, move so Mo can come in the house," I said.

"You can't come in my house," Ace said. He attempted to close the door in Mo's face, but was stopped when I put my hand in the way.

"What are you doing? Let her in," I replied for Mo.

"She can't come in my house and if that's a problem for you, you can take yo' ass with her," Ace replied, giving me an ultimatum.

"Are you serious right now?" I questioned.

Ace opened the door up all the way and walked away. Scooting back in the wheelchair, I looked up trying to figure out why Ace's sister is still standing here.

"Are you and Tee Tee going to stay here?" Mo questioned, checking her phone. Looking over, Dani was still standing there looking at me.

"Damn, do you mind?" I questioned.

"Yea, I do. This is my brother's house and I can stand anywhere I want to in here," Dani replied with a smirk.

"Dani, get the fuck out her face before you get put the fuck out!" Ace yelled from a distance.

"What the fuck is going on between you and him?" I asked once Dani made her way down the hallway taking her slow, sweet, precious time.

"He had something to do with Big Face getting locked up," Mo replied, rolling her eyes.

"He wouldn't do that," I assured Mo.

"You don't know what he'd do," Mo replied with an attitude.

"Y'all staying here?" Mo asked again like she was in a hurry and had somewhere to go.

Honk! Honk! Honk! Somebody blew their horn repeatedly in front of Ace's home. Looking in the direction of the car, I saw Ace's aunt getting out the car. I'd rather not deal with this bitch today; as if I already don't have enough shit going on. By the look on her face, she was just as unpleased to see me.

"Come on, Mo, we need to go," Joy said.

"Since when did you start hanging out with her?" I asked as Joy walked around me and made her way in the house.

"I'm goin' with her to talk to Big Face's lawyer," Mo admitted as her phone rang.

"Why?"

Something in my wheelchair started vibrating. Feeling around, I found my phone in a pocket and I had a text message from Kai.

Kai: If you need anything, call me, Mina. Your brother is just upset. Just give him some time. Every—

I stopped reading her text and pressed the side button on

my phone, locking it. Mo didn't respond to my question and Joy brushed past me making her way back out the house.

"It's nothin' like that. She just asked me to go with her," Mo finally said, slipping her phone into her back pocket.

"Clearly she doesn't think that Ace had anything to do with Big Face being locked up."

"She doesn't know what happened," Mo whispered, like someone was listening.

"Call me when you're done and we'll be ready to go with you," I said.

"She ain't goin' with you," Ace said from behind me, pushing my chair and slamming the door in Mo's face swiftly.

"Why would you do that? Me and Tiana are staying with her until I figure some things out," I admitted.

"Get ready, they are coming for you next!" Mo screamed from the other side of the door.

"Bitch, they will come for yo' klepto' ass before they come for me!" Ace screamed, opening the door, so everybody that was listening could hear him.

"Why the fuck would you say that?" I yelled, waking up Tiana.

"Fuck her," Ace replied, shutting the door and pushing us down the hallway.

"Why is she saying that you have something to do with Big Face being locked up?"

"Because she doesn't know what the fuck she is talking about," Ace responded, leaving me wondering what the fuck Mo knows that would have her questioning Ace's loyalty to his right-hand.

We made it to the living room where Dani and Zay were sitting on the couch. The TV was so loud that my ears started to ring. Ace snatched up the remote and turned it down as Tiana started to whine. Ace wasted no time taking her out my lap. If we could have some privacy, so that we could talk, it would be nice. Dani was just staring at me, not saying anything. I was impatiently waiting for Ace to tell her to give us a minute.

"Ace, we need—" I attempted to say before he cut me off.

"Dani, give us a minute," Ace said, talking to her but looking at me.

"For what?" Dani questioned with her attitude evident.

"Do you want to be homeless?" Ace asked.

"For this bitch?" Dani asked, pointing at me.

"Call her another bitch and yo' ass will be back at crack alley," Ace said, causing Dani to storm out the room with Zay close behind.

"That wasn't necessary," I said as I heard Dani and Zay stomping up the stairs.

"What do you want to talk about?" Ace asked as he played with Tiana.

"Are you still fuckin' with Jessica?" I asked.

"You for real right now?"

"Yes, I want to know," I demanded, folding my arms over my chest.

"That's the first thing that you want to say to a nigga? That's what the fuck you want to talk about so bad, nigga? Jessica? Fuck that bitch. I was fuckin' her, not fuckin' with he—"

"What the fuck is the difference?" I questioned, cutting him off.

"We were fuckin', nothing more and nothing less, Ahmina."

"You think that's okay?"

"I didn't say that it was okay. Did I? You asked a question, so I gave you an answer. What the fuck you want me to do, lie to you? I ain't that nigga and I ain't gon' be for you!" Ace spat coldly.

"What the fuck is wrong with you? You think it's okay to talk to me like this?" I asked, confused. This is not what I imagined our reunion would be like.

2

ACE

Looking at Mina and the tears welling up in her eyes, I didn't know what to say. I want her here, that's why I didn't let her leave with Modesty. The more we sit here just looking at each other, the more it sank in that a nigga can't do nothin' for her, let alone Tee Tee. With my current position, I can't bring her into this shit with me. But her being here now, how the fuck am I going to tell her to leave.? I didn't think the day would come that I would see her again. With Mo being on her bullshit, I didn't even know what her current state was.

All a nigga been doing is hittin' licks. I still got a lil money saved up, but not enough to last me long. And now with my sister being back in the picture, I need to be able to make sure that she is good too. I damn sure don't want her at my house, but I would rather her be here than to be at OG's stressing her. I have to lock up everything in my house and watch her like a fuckin' little kid.

I jumped up from the couch with Tee Tee still in my arms and made my way upstairs to go and check on Dani. Every so often, I count her ass like she in jail because I'll look up and her ass been done tried to rob me for what the fuck I got left.

"Ace!" Mina yelled out, but I didn't answer.

"Why are y'all in my room?" I asked, causing Zay to jump, but Dani just kept watching TV like I wasn't talking to her ass.

I stood at the foot of the bed staring at Dani, waiting for her to get her punk ass out my bed with all her fuckin' snacks stretched out over my bed. My phone vibrated as Tee Tee started waving at Dani and Zay. Zay responded to her, but Dani didn't even acknowledge her, causing me to get more agitated.

"Muthafucka, I know you hear her and see her. Get the fuck out my room, Dani," I demanded, answering my phone.

"Nigga, that's not your daughter," Dani said, getting up and gathering all her shit up.

"Wassup, OG?" I asked into the phone.

"Why you over here trying to play daddy to that lil girl, you need to be over there checking on Tamera!" Dani screamed loud enough for Mina to hear her.

"This ain't gon' work," I said to my momma, referring to Dani being over here.

"Make it work. Now, what is this Joy saying that Mina and her daughter is over there?" OG questioned.

I know that Annie didn't even get off the street good before she called my momma to tell her that Mina was over here. I've never discussed what was goin' on between me and Kurupt with my momma, but she knows that something is going on for sure because of how I've been moving. Not to mention, she knew what happened with Mina. She always asks, but I never respond. And when I do, I always tell her that I got us, we'll be good and nothing else. I've never discussed my business with her and I'm not going to start now.

"Aiden, I know that you hear me," OG said as Dani finally gathered up all her shit.

"Stay the fuck out of my room or sleep in the park, the choice is yours!" I spat after muting my phone, so OG wouldn't hear me.

"Aiden!" OG screamed in my ear.

"Yes, OG, I'm here."

"You need to get that girl out of that house."

"OG, I'll be over to talk to you in a few hours."

"You got an hour."

Click.

I made my way around my room after checking all of my hiding spots, making sure that my safe is locked then made my way out of my room. It's a fucked-up feeling knowing that you got to check all yo' shit, but with my sister, I don't have any other choice. If she'd steal from my momma, she damn sure don't mind stealing from me. I made my way down the hall to the guest room where Zay and Dani had been sleeping. Zay was knocked out. Dani looked at me, rolled her eyes and turned up the volume on the TV like I wanted to talk to her ass.

Tee Tee fell asleep in my arms and as I walked down the stairs, all I could hear was Tee's snores. I can't even hear the TV down here. When I walked into the living room, Ahmina was still in the same place that I left her.

"So, you want me to stay here, but you're not going to talk to me? What did I do to you?" Mina cried out.

I pulled Tee Tee's cover out of her bag, spread it over the couch and laid Tee Tee down. I made my way back over to Mina and pulled her wheelchair over to me, so that she was facing me. Wiping Mina's tears away, I handed her some tissue.

"Mina, what do you want a nigga to say? I'm fucked up. A nigga can barely make sure that I'm good," I admitted. Saying that shit to Mina and the look on her face just made a nigga feel worse than I already did.

As Mina stared at me looking for a nigga to have the answers and a solution for what the fuck were going to do, I started thinking about my OG and Annie. Shit, Big Face too, even though his bitch got me fucked up. I can't even talk to him because Iman advised me it's best that we don't communicate. I told Iman everything that I needed him to tell Big Face, but with the evidence they found, who knows how the fuck this is going to play out.

"I gave up everything that I know. I went against my brother, the only family that I have, to be here right now. I'm not asking you to take care of me and Tianna, that isn't yo' responsibility."

I didn't know what to say because right now, I can't do shit for her. And fucking with her in her current state is my fault and has put me in a position where I'm back to square one. We were just staring at each other, but neither one of us said anything else. I never wanted to put Ahmina in the position that she's in now. I'm just waiting for her to say something about Tamera.

"I have to go and talk to my OG. Do you need anything before I leave?" I asked, standing up from the couch.

"Yea, for you to tell me who the fuck is Tamera?" Mina questioned.

"Jessica and yo' baby daddy's daughter. Any more fucking questions?"

She scooted her chair back away from me. I walked around her and made my way upstairs to get my keys and tool, so I could go listen to whatever it is that my OG has to say. My family has always said that Tamera looks like me. They wanted Tamera to be mine, so they would say anything to get me to fuck with her. My momma wanted me to be with her so damn bad. My momma doesn't know the real her and if she did, she wouldn't feel the way that she does.

I LOOKED up and down the block to see if I saw anybody that shouldn't be here, but I didn't. Everybody that I see lives here or is always over here. I opened the door and a car damn near side swiped my door. Gripping my tool, I made my way into the house. A few niggas spoke and I nodded my head and kept it the fuck moving. I didn't have shit to say to anybody, so when D was running over, I slammed the porch door and locked it as he came in the fence.

"Why are you slamming my door, Aiden?" OG asked as I walked in the front door.

"My bad," I said as D started knocking on the door.

"Let me go and get the door," OG said as I stopped her from going to the door.

"I got it."

I made my way out the front door and closed it. And just like I knew she would, my OG opened the door and came out on the porch to speak to D. I haven't talked to this nigga in months and we don't have shit to talk about now. I'm not gon' be as harsh as Big Face, but I ain't got shit for him. I don't have shit for nobody.

"Alright, OG, naw, he ain't hungry. He just ate," I said because she getting being too damn friendly.

"How do you know he just ate? He looks a lil hungry," OG said.

"Naw, I'm good. Thank you doe," D said.

"Nigga, what do you want?" I asked before OG could make it in the house good.

"Man, I know it's been a minute since we talked 'bout shit. I was able to get shit together and I'm all the way right," D pleade,d rubbing his hands together.

"How many percs you had today?"

"Hun?"

"How many percs have you had today?"

"Man, you know me. That ain't gon' stop me from putting in work."

This nigga in my face looking like he ain't slept in weeks. He been hanging around with them lil niggas, so he just out here poppin' pills and drinking every day. He left that bitch alone because she left him alone, so he had no choice. It wasn't like he got some fucking sense and left the bitch alone. If she call that nigga right now, he gon' run to her.

"I can't help you, nigga. You see what I'm driving. Nigga, look at me," I said as he looked me up and down then looked back up at me like he was feeling sorry for me.

I admit, I let myself go. I ain't had a haircut since the day that Mina got hit by that car, and I ain't been myself since that day either. I sold my car to get some money to keep shit going and get some work from this off-brand nigga Tone. His shit ain't Kurupt's, but it's been working. I lost the trap because I couldn't pay that rent and mine. Shit, until I get back right. I need to move in here, but my momma don't want Danni in her house, yet I'm supposed to house the hoe in mine.

"I see some shit done changed, but nigga, you know me and you know that I got you. I can do whatever and I know that I fucked up, but I'm ready to make shit right," D said.

"Go to rehab or get yo' self together then come and talk to me," I said, thinking about the fact that D's sister's spot would be the perfect place to move shit out of.

"Why were you talking to that boy like that? You been friends with that boy damn near yo whole life. Everybody goes through rough times. You can't give up on people when they are going through it," OG lectured as I walked through the door.

I didn't waste my time responding because she'll never understand. I made my way to the kitchen to get something to eat because I know my momma cooked. She was on my heels and I was glad. mWe needed to talk and get this over with, so I can get back to my house to watch my sister.

"What's up, OG?" I said as she set down at the kitchen table and I made a plate.

"Why would you let that girl and her daughter come to your house? What about us and our safety? You're willing to risk that for her?" OG questioned.

"She showed up at the house. I didn't even know that she had woken up. I care about Mina, OG."

"That boy can kill us all, then what?"

"He ain't thinking about that!" Annie yelled as she came into the kitchen.

"I'm starting to think that you not, Aiden. Have you called your father back?" OG questioned like it's not enough going on.

"OG, I'm not answering his calls. We don't have nothing to talk about. And to be honest, now is not the time that I want to discuss him," I replied. I'm sick of her bringing that nigga up.

When she first gave him my number and I answered not knowing who it was, I blocked his ass. We don't have shit to discuss. I love and respect my momma, but she is putting me in a position with that nigga that I don't like. She should just respect how I feel about him and leave it alone, but every time I turn around, she's bringing him up. My momma never was the type to dog out my father or to bring other niggas around. If she did ever deal with anybody after him, I never seen or heard about them.

"Was that all you wanted to talk about?" I asked OG as her and Annie just looked at me crazy.

They know how I feel about them. Everything that I do is to make sure that they are good. The fact that OG is questioning that had me mad as hell. Annie doesn't like anybody, so the fact that she is acting the way that she is doesn't surprise me. All of a sudden, her and Modesty are the best of friends, but she had an issue with Mina before she ever met her.

"Annie, what's yo problem?" I asked. I know half the reason why OG has anything to say is because of whatever she is telling her.

"You don't need that girl anywhere near you," Annie finally said.

"Annie, I know what I need to do. I don't need to hear yo' opinion right no—"

"Now, all of a fucking sudden you don't need my opinion. What the fuck is going on with you? You need to get yo' self together and be a fucking man! Do you know how many bitches is out here? You trippin' about one like she somethin' fuckin' special."

"OG, I'll call you," I said. I took my last bite and put my plate in the sink.

OG just started shaking her head. Ever since that nigga that fucked us over that she wants me to talk to so damn bad, I've been taking care of myself. Robbing and stealing to make sure that we were good. I never got to enjoy my childhood because I had to do shit to survive.

They not thinking about all the shit that I made possible. If it wasn't for me, we wouldn't be sitting in this house; who knows where the fuck we would be. I don't get credit for none of that. They just so damn concerned with Mina. Annie was talking shit, but after her comment about being a man, I was done listening to anything that she had to say. Her and her son on some bullshit. When Big Face and me have a disagreement, she always stays neutral , but I can tell by her attitude and the way she moving that she got a fucking attitude and is feeling some type of way. I'm sure that hanging around that bitch Mina didn't make it any better.

"You might as well just gon' head and send Bri and Zay over here because I don't want nothing to happen to them behind you," Annie said as I turned to leave.

Looking back at my OG and how she was looking Annie upside her head, I knew she didn't want Bri over here. If that was the case, she would have never told me that I needed to keep her over here. OG doesn't even want Bri to come over here and visit, which I don't blame her because of all the hoe shit that she has done over the years.

"Aiden, please be careful," OG pleaded. I nodded my head and made my way out the house.

Looking up and down the street, I waited until the car that just drove by disappeared into the darkness until I stepped off the porch. I haven't seen or heard anything from Kurupt and his people. That doesn't mean that they aren't somewhere lurkin' in the shadows or got some of their people watching a nigga.

Pop! Pop! Pop! Rat-tat-tat-tat!

Bullets started flying. As I pulled my tool out to bust back, OG's front window shattered. All I could hear was them screaming and multiple guns firing in my direction.

3

MINA

"How long have you been talking to my brother?" Dani asked from behind me like she really gave a fuck.

I shut the bathroom door and rolled back the living room, ignoring her. I want to know what is taking Ace so long to get back. He's been gone for damn near five hours. I keep calling his phone and it's going straight to the voicemail. I never knew she even existed, so she damn sure can't be too important. All he ever talked about or seemed to care about to me was his OG and Annie's rude ass, so I don't know where she came from. This bitch could be playing a role and be a whole bitch for all I know.

"Umm, did you hear me? Are you deaf and cripple?" Dani joked, but I didn't find shit funny.

"Ha ha ha... That's not fucking funny. Any questions that you have, you need to direct them to Ace because I don't know you," I spat as I struggled to get out of my chair and onto the couch next to where Tianna is sleeping.

My phone started vibrating and I knew it was nobody but Kai. I know that she wants to help and all, but she needs to just give me some space and time to think. Shit, Kurupt ain't thinking about my ass. Looking at my phone, it was a number that I don't know. They had called a few times while I was in the bathroom. They didn't leave a message but the sent three text messages.

720-312-9985: Baby

720-312-9985: I know that you been around that hoe ass nigga, but I'm coming home.

720-312-9985: I know that I fucked up and made some mistakes, but I want to make shit right. I know what I need to do and I'm going to do whatever it takes to make things right again between us. You didn't deserve what I put you through. All the things that you wanted I'm going to make sure that you get it. My only concern is coming home to you and my baby. I love you!

I'm not surprised that Tycoon is texting me. This shit about him getting out is what I want to know about. The days of me wanting him to do right and for us to be a family are behind us. I don't want anything from him and Tianna is better off without him. I won't stop him from being a part of her life, but me and him are never going to be.

"I'm just gone tell my brother that you are texting yo' baby daddy," Dani sang as she walked around the couch.

"Girl, leave me the fuck alone," I spat, making Tati jump in her sleep.

"Give me fifty dollars and I will," Dani requested, holding out her hand.

I picked up my phone and started scrolling through Instagram. I saw that Kai had just posted pictures of the twins. They had gotten so big. I feel like I've missed out on so much time. I kept checking my call log to see if Kurupt has tried to call me, but he hasn't. My phone started ringing and this crazy bitch was straining her neck with her hand still out trying to see who it is. I turned my screen to her, so she could see that it is my dad.

"Hello," I said as I answered.

"Baby girl, why did you leave the house? Where are you and Tiana at?" My father asked.

"We are good."

"I didn't ask you that, Ahmina. You need to be with your family and where you are able to be monitored. The doctors told Kurupt that you still need to be watched. Not only did you just get out of an a coma, Ahmina, you're pregnant. This isn't about you. This is about the baby. I'm getting on a flight and coming to get y'all."

"No, we're good."

"Ahmina, did you hear anything that I just said to you?"

"I'll call you back later," I said and hung up.

I wasn't trying to forget the fact that I was pregnant, but right now is not the best time to bring a baby into the world. I'm homeless and Ace is just one lick away from being homeless his damn self. I would turn my phone off but I need to be able to answer if Ace calls because he still hasn't made it back here. Looking up from my phone, Dani was still in my face and pissing me off. If I could get up like I want to, I would beat her ass.

"Just give me twenty?" Dani bargained.

"Bitch, are you smoking?" I questioned, becoming even more irritated.

"Get yo' shit and get the fuck out!" Ace's aunt Joy screamed at the top of lungs as she came rushing into the living room.

"I'm not going anywhere. You might not like the fact that I'm here, but Ace's wants me here or I wouldn't be here," I said, picking up Tiana and putting her in her lap because she's damn sure up now.

"Well, right now Ace is laid in hospital bed and my sister is a few rooms down thanks to you. So you can either get in that wheelchair and get the fuck out on yo' own or I will remove yo' ass. The choice is yours!" Joy screamed.

"Annie, what are you talking about? What happened to my momma and brother?" Dani cried out.

"Did you make up yo' muthafuckin' mind because time is up?" Joy questioned as she went to grab my wheelchair.

I found strength I didn't know I had and snatched it back from her. We didn't bring shit with us, but some of Tiana's stuff. I sat Tiana down beside me and got in my chair as they gawked. It was so quiet int the room that you could hear a penny drop. I had a lot to say, but I was more concerned with what was going on with Ace. Clearly, I'm not going to get any information from them. I picked up Tiana and made my way to the front door. A man saw me struggling to get my chair over the door and keep me and Tiana in the chair with tears running down my face.

"Hold on, I'll help you. Let me call you right back," a man called out as he jogged over to help me.

I never needed something so simple in my life, and for it to have to come from a stranger while two bitter bitches just stared and whispered among themselves. Before I could thank the man that came to help me, Joy slammed the front door in our faces.

"Damn, are you alright? Where is Ace?" The man questioned.

"I don't know, I'm good. I'm going to call a ride, but thank you," I managed to say as I wiped my tears away and called Mo.

Mo's phone rang and eventually went to the voicemail, so I tried again after ignoring my dad's phone call. Where the fuck is Mo? Why isn't she answering the phone? She already seen how shit was before she left, so she really needs to answer the phone. I tried again, but she didn't answer.

"Is that her?" I heard somebody ask.

"She looks like the girl in the picture?" Somebody yelled back.

"Hey, what's up?" A man awkwardly asked as he walked up on me and Tiana.

I acted like I didn't hear him and tried to call Mo again. After a few rings, she didn't answer, so I dialed Murk's number. Maybe she's with him and if she's not, I'm going to go down the list and call everybody else that she might be with. Why the fuck isn't she answering the phone? My phone started vibrating in my hand. Looking at the preview of the text, I saw it' was Lady H. I knew she was only calling because I hung up on my dad and was ignoring him. She's across the country, so right now she can't be any of assistance.

"Umm, look. You have to come with us," the nigga requested.

"I'm not going with no fucking body!" I screamed, causing a scene, hoping one of these nosy muthafuckas called the damn police, started recording or something. They been all in the business since I was trying to get out the front door and it seems like the whole damn neighborhood is out here now.

The man didn't seem phased by my comments and was now on the phone talking to somebody. This isn't somebody that works for Kurupt because I know all of them. He wouldn't send anybody to get me if he wanted me. I don't know who the fuck this man is, but I'm not going anywhere with him.

"Look, let's not make this harder than it has to be. I had clear instructions for you to come with me, so just come on," the man requested, trying to take Tiana out of my lap.

"Don't touch my fucking daughter!" I spat. Another nigga ran over to where we were.

"Why the fuck can't I just knock this bitch out again?" The nigga that had been trying to get me to come with him questioned.

It was dark out and the only light is the lights coming from people's porch lights, phones and the streetlights which isn't enough clearly for these nosy muthafuckas to see that I need some fucking assistance. I'm running out of time and options, so I did the last thing that I could think of.

"Help! Help! I don't know these men. They are trying to kind—" I yelled as loud as I could and the muthafuckas started making their way in their fucking houses like I wasn't begging for help.

Me crying and yelling, on top of Tiana screaming bloody murder, wasn't a cry for help in this neighborhood I see. None of these muthafuckas even budged. I looked around to see if I saw the nigga that helped me get over the threshold, but I didn't see him anymore.

"We gon' have to pick her up," one of the niggas suggested. I prayed as I dialed 911 under the cover that was draped over Tiana and me.

"Muthafucka, you get her legs," the nigga that that was losing his patience said, flicking his cigarette.

"Put me down! Help! Help!" I cried out.

"Girl ain't nobody kidnapping you, shut the fuck up!" One of the men barked. He tied something over my mouth so fast that I couldn't have stop him as bad as I wanted to.

4

BIG FACE

"What are you doing here, Brionna?" I asked, looking around because my momma was supposed to be coming to get me.

"I came because yo' mom couldn't, nigga. You could always walk if you don't want to ride with me. I'm not in the mood for yo' shit today," Bri said, adjusting her glasses on her face.

I know that nigga Bad News be kicking her ass, but that's her business. It stopped being my business what she did and how she was moving when she stopped being my bitch. I can't be worried about her, if she ain't and right now, the only muthafucka that I'm worried about is myself.

"Good because I don't want to hear yo' shit today. Tina, take me to OG's," I said as I got in her truck.

"You can't go there," Bri said as I pulled off.

"What the fuck do you mean I can't go there?" I questioned as I powered my phone on.

"For real, nigga?" A familiar voice yelled as I rolled the passenger side window down to get a good look at Modesty.

"You're not my bitch. I never even fucked you and here you go stalking me already. I told yo ass when you showed up to the jail with my momma to fall back."

Before Mo could respond, Bri slammed on the gas and left Modesty sitting there. I didn't give a fuck about that. Being out is the only thing that I'm concerned about and why the fuck my momma didn't come and pick me up. Bri had an attitude when she picked me up and Modesty only made it worse.

"So, you gon' tell me what the fuck is going on?" I asked as Bri turned the corner like she had lost her fucking mind.

"Ask that bitch," Bri said and turned up the music.

"Brionna, what's my name?" I asked as I turned the radio all the way off.

"Nigga, what?"

"What the fuck is my name?"

"Caleb," she finally responded.

"You didn't get amnesia while I was away, so stop fucking playing with me and tell me what the fuck is going on. Where the fuck is my momma and why can't I go to OG's? That's where the fuck them people think that I'm going to be staying at."

The only reason why they let me out is because I don't have any priors and overcrowding in the jail. If it wasn't for that, my black ass would be in jail. I know that my momma told Brionna all my business, so I don't know why the fuck she hasn't told me yet. Bri had tried to visit me while I was in jail. When I walked to the camera and seen it was her, I walked away without even picking up the phone, not once, but twice. When she started fucking with that nigga Big Face, she made her decision and that was the end of us. But for some reason, she won't let a nigga go.

This bitch is driving crazy as hell. Swerving in and out of lanes in this big ass truck. Almost hitting muthafuckas and all types of shit. I'm surprised that we ain't got pulled over with how she is fucking driving. Any time that I talk to Bri or am around her, she always has an attitude; I haven't seen her happy in years. I haven't seen her smile or fucking laugh in about a year. She thought that nigga was the best thing in the world when she first started fucking with him, but now she just stuck and miserable because she knows that she can't come back to me.

"What the fuck is wrong with you? You on yo' period?" I asked.

"Fuck you, Caleb," she replied.

"What the fuck is wrong with you? If that damn unhappy, you need to leave that nigga. You got the keys to the house, still go there," I suggested.

"Get the fuck out my truck!" Bri yelled, slamming on her breaks.

"Bitch, that nigga must have hit you in yo' head too many times. You not about to just kick me out this truck. I'll bust all the windows out this bitch. Man, just take me to the house and quit playin' with me, Brionna!"

"This is where yo' momma and everybody else is at," Bri yelled back and jumped when I unbuckled my seatbelt like I was going to hit her.

I jumped out the truck, leaving her door open. Fuck that bitch and that door. I made my way into the hospital while calling my momma for the hundredth time. What the fuck is going on? I know that it's not my momma in the hospital, I talked to her earlier. And if she was, Brionna would have had her big forehead ass in here. She thinks my momma is hers for some fucking reason.

"What the fuck is going on?" I asked as I walked up on Dani and Zay in the waiting room.

"Somebody shot up momma's house, and her and Ace were hit," Dani said as my mom whispered to somebody on the phone.

"Who are you talking to that you couldn't answer my phone calls?" I asked, not even acknowledging what Dani just said.

"Caleb, I'm yo' momma, you ain't mine."

"Yea, whatever. I don't care what is going on. I don't want

Brionna nowhere near me. You need to quit talking to that bitch," I said as I sat down next to Dani.

"You don't get to tell me who the fuck I can or cannot talk to. Just shut the fuck up and quit talking to me," my momma replied and busted out crying.

Dani tried to console her, but she pushed her off and made her way down the hall. I wasn't even going to attempt to try. I know my momma and she ain't gone do nothing but fight anybody. The only person that could possibly try and calm her down is OG, and she laid up in the hospital. Not because of the cancer that has been the cause in the past, but bullets that were meant for Ace and me. Pulling out my wallet, I pulled out a card of the case manager that I met with earlier to let her know that I was at the hospital.

She didn't answer, so I left a message. I got this big ass GPS box on, so the bitch can see exactly where the fuck I'm at. I just knew that I was going home to go to sleep. I was going to call a bitch to come over, but it wasn't neither one of the bitches I done seen so far.

"You want to go back and see Ace?" Dani asked.

"Naw, I'm good," I replied.

"What the fuck do you mean you good? Take yo' ass back there and see him and OG," My momma demanded as she walked back over to where we were sitting.

I didn't even waste my time responding because I'm not going back there. The last time that I was in this hospital, my son was back there in one of the rooms and he didn't come up out this bitch, so I'm not going back there to see no fucking body. The only muthafucka that I would call to come and pick me up done already pissed me off, so I ain't calling her back up here. Looking at Dani, she ain't no fucking help. That bitch don't got a bike let alone a car. All crackheads at least got a bike; this bitch is sorry as hell.

"Where the fuck is you going?" My momma asked.

"The fuck out of here," I replied.

"OG IS AWAKE, MUTHAFUCKA!" My momma barked, causing me to rollover in my sleep.

"Muthafucka, did you hear me? My sister is alive not that you give a fuck since you couldn't even take yo' black ass back there to see about her. You a sorry muthafucka!" My momma yelled loud enough for the neighbors to hear as I wiped my eyes.

"You already know how I feel about the fucking hospital. You knew I wasn't going back there when Dani asked did I want to. If that bitch was ever around, she would have known not to even ask me."

"What the fuck did Bri do to you? It's not bad enough that you didn't call her while you were locked up. Then you had the nerve to refuse her visits. Who the fuck do you think you is?"

"Momma, I do not fuck with Brionna like that. Brionna is not my bitch, I don't have to call her. I didn't do shit to that bitch."

"Well, she's pregnant," my momma threw in there.

"What the fuck are you telling me for? I give all my spare change and ones to the homeless. That is all the charity that a nigga can give anybody, so I really don't know what the fuck you telling me that bitch is pregnant for." I asked. I got up even more irritated than I was before I went to sleep and made my way into the bathroom.

"Do you hear that?" My momma asked as she started banging in the bathroom door.

I acted like I didn't hear her. I heard some bitch outside screaming my name. I heard that shit before I went to sleep and right now, I don't have no time to give no bitch nothing but dick. I think I know who it is, but I didn't even waste my time looking out the window. I didn't call none of them bitches when I was locked up because I didn't want none of the them to think a damn thing changed. You call a bitch once while you locked up and they think y'all in a whole fucking relationship, putting all that shit all over Facebook.

I finished handling my business and made my way out that bathroom. My momma was still at the bathroom door talking shit.

"You need to get yo' shit together. You done put Brionna through enough. She needs you to be there for her!" My momma yelled.

"You be there for her because that ain't my baby, and she can't get nothing else from me. She made her choice when she started fucking with that nigga. I don't know why you believe that she pregnant by me. She might want it to be my baby, but that's her nigga baby. Look, I know that you want another grand baby, but right now that ain't gone happen. Be her baby play grandma."

"I don't know which one of them dumb ass bitches you think you talking to, but you need to remember who the fuck you talking to. I got one daughter, nigga, and yo' muthafuckin' ass ain't her!"

"Aight, momma," I said and walked away from her because she not trying to hear nothing that I just said.

My phone started ringing. Checking the caller id, it was my sister. I'm surprised that my momma even referred to her as her daughter because she hasn't talked to her in years. They have always had a fucked-up relationship. My sister was damn near just as bad as Dani, but her addiction was niggas, not crack. That's why her ass is locked up now.

"Wassup, Nia," I said as the call connected.

"Where the fuck you been at? I been calling you," Nia questioned.

"Shit, I got locked up. What's up? You good?" I asked.

Me and Nia caught up. Nia is older than me. She's thirty something and she can't get herself together. This last time she got jammed up, my momma just gave up on her. Between me and Nia, we gave my momma hell. She always babied me, but she stayed on Nia's ass. That shit didn't work.

"How's momma doing?" Nia asked.

"She alright, still in my damn business," I said loud enough for my momma to hear and she threw a bottle of my cologne off the dresser in my direction.

"Don't tell can't get right none of my damn business!" My momma yelled like we weren't in the same room.

I moved just in time for it to not hit me. Nia ain't gone ever change, but she's my sister. I'll body a nigga about her and a bitch too. Nia should be coming home soon. I say soon because she can't do right in the pin either. She always in some shit and it's never her fault because she's always down for the wrong muthafuckas.

"You and Bri back together yet?" Dani asked like I knew she would.

"You talk to that bitch every day, so I know that you know that bitch fuck with that other nigga," I replied.

"You pick and choose when you want to fuck with her. I know that you never gon' change. You gon' always have all them bitches, but you really loved Bri at one point. You didn't treat her the way that you treated them hoes," Nia said, knowing both sides.

"Only a hoe would tell another hoe that it's okay to be a hoe!" My momma screamed loud enough for Nia to hear.

"She always got something to say. She wasn't always in the house taking care of OG!" Nia yelled in my ear.

"Nigga, my ear!"

"Shut up, crybaby ass nigga. I need you to do me a favor," Nia whined.

"What, Nia? I'm not calling that hoe ass nig—" I attempted to say before my momma cut me off.

"A real nigga would make sure that you're okay! A real nigga would be there for you and you wouldn't be depending on Caleb to make sure that you're good! A real nigga would be there for you in any way possible! You wouldn't have to have another muthafucka call them to get them to answer your calls!" My momma yelled.

"You might as well talk to her if you got all that to say!"

"Oooh, I can't stand her. I need you to call this number and do one more thing for me Big Face!" Nia screamed.

"You worse than Red crazy ass that's outside screaming my name," I said as I got up, looking out the window to see who the fuck it was. "Alright, Nia hold on. Bitch, get away from my fucking house. You a crazy stalker, bitch! Bitch, you on punishment indefinitely!" I yelled out the window at Red's crazy ass.

"Look, I know y'all fucked up. I got this money on the floor. Shit is right, I promise."

"Who am I calling?" I asked, intrigued, opening my safe and looking at how my stash is dwindling down.

"Daddy Vino," Nia sang.

"Bitch, I ain't calling no nigga daddy! What the fuck is his name?"

"Sevino."

5

MODESTY

"What do you want Murk?" I groggily asked.

"Why the fuck you ain't answering the phone?" Murk questioned.

"Did you pay Sprint?"

"Probably muthafucka. Get up and answer the door!" Murk spat.

"I'm not at home," I lied.

"Quit playing with me, Modesty. Where the fuck are you at then?"

"I'll get with you lat—"

"You gon' quit talking to me like I'm some bitch ass nigga. Get up and open the door before I bust out the windows in this fucking truck, Modesty."

"You better not touch my fucking truck, Murk!" I yelled, getting up to let this crazy muthafucka in the building.

My remote to the garage isn't working, so I had to park on the street. His crazy stalking ass and bitches is why I don't like parking on the street. I have been ignoring him. The problems that I'm having, he can't do shit for me. I haven't wasted my time answering his phone calls because I don't want to be bothered. But, he's the type of nigga that will pop up. That's exactly why I didn't want him to know where I lived, but he followed me home one night when I left from him.

"Do I just pop up at yo' house?" I asked as I swung open my front door.

"Move out of my way," Murk spat and pushed past me, damn near knocking me down.

"Don't come in here with all that, you could have stayed where the fuck you were at. I don't have time for yo' attitude today."

Murk came right on in, went straight to the kitchen, then grabbed a Pepsi out of the icebox and my bag of hot Cheetos off the counter. He flopped down on my couch and kicked up his feet like he was at home. Murk is cool and all, but it just would never work. How do you go from being a trick and being cool with that for years to all of sudden you want to be in a relationship? I don't know where that bitch is at that he was fucking with, but he needs to go find her and get her back before I go and find her for him.

"Sit down," Murk said, patting on the couch next to him.

"Nigga, I know that you passed at least five seven elevens on the way from Nanny's house," I replied, irritated that he just decided to eat my damn Cheetos.

"Don't call my grandma nanny, she ain't yo' damn grandma. What, you back chasing that nigga Big Face?"

"Nigga, fuck you and ya grandma, get out," I said. As soon as the words left my mouth, I regretted it.

Murk jumped up and was on my ass, pushing me into the wall, grabbing me by my throat as I tried to pry his hands from around my neck.

"You need to watch yo' fucking mouth. You always have to go too far. Shut the fuck up sometimes. I play about a lot of shit, but don't say shit in reference to my fucking grandma!" Murk spat, still not letting go of my neck.

"Maurice, stop," I managed to say, but it was like he didn't hear me because he didn't give a fuck or let up.

"Stupid ass," Mark spat as he banged my head into the wall just when I thought that I was about to pass the fuck out.

My head hitting the wall hard as hell woke my ass up. He walked back over to the couch like it was nothing, flopped back down and started swiping through his phone. I got up and made my way to the bathroom. He didn't give a fuck and kept doing what he was doing on his phone. This isn't the first time that Murk has put his hands on me. It isn't something that he does all the time but say the wrong thing to his ass or do some shit that he ain't okay with and the consequence may be that you have to duck and dodge a few punches or get choked the fuck out like what he just did.

I looked at my neck and as black as I am, I can still see where his hands had been around my neck. Looking up, I saw him in the bathroom mirror standing behind me. He didn't said nothing but just looked at me.

"Why you can't just do the right thing? What type of woman want to run around fucking all these different niggas?" Murk asked, breaking the silence between us.

"If I'm such a horrible woman, why the fuck do you keep coming back?" I asked.

"Modesty, I'm not about to keep playing these games with you. You're going to have to figure out what you want."

"What I don't want is Ike Turner."

"Then learn to shut the fuck up sometimes. Don't talk to a nigga like I just go upside yo' fucking head for no reason. I don't give a fuck what you say about me, but you ain't have to bring nanny into it."

Nanny hates my ass. Murk always trying to get me to come

around her and or to come to his sister Masika's house, but I won't. After the few times that I went around her, I know that they didn't want me there, and I don't go places that I'm not wanted. Nanny didn't mind making it known that she wanted that girl that Murk was fucking with to be at her house not me. It was cool. I understand the bitch take yo' old ass to the grocery store and to get yo' nails done. I'm not the bitch that's going to be doing none of that.

Murk walked away because he knew that I wasn't about to say what he wanted to hear. He's not used to people telling him no. Nanny is always babying that nigga. She raised him and his sister from the day they left the hospital. His momma lives three houses down from where Nanny used to live and lived there their whole life, but never even acknowledged them. Masika is a square and doesn't do anything but work and go to school. Murk jumped in the streets with Envii and has never looked back.

I heard my phone ringing in the other room, but it's stopped. I rolled my eyes as I heard Murk talking to whoever is calling me. I washed my face and brushed my teeth then made my way back to the living room to get my phone.

"What do you mean she's missing?" Murk asked.

I didn't even bother asking why he was answering my phone because he doesn't give a fuck who it was calling, this nigga was going to answer. Murk has been there for me when I needed him, but we would never work. How you start is how you finish. He started off as a trick and that is what he will always be to me. He needs to find somebody that can deal with his anger and mommy issues, but that bitch ain't me.

"Nigga, she's missing and Kai hasn't talked to her or been able to text her in two days. The police came to the house saying that they got a call from a number that is registered in K's fucking name, but when they arrived at the address that it linked them to, they weren't able to find the phone, her or get any answers from the fucking neighbors! Where the fuck is Modesty!" Envii screamed once Murk put her on speaker phone.

"Just calm down, Envii," Kai suggested, letting me know that she was on the phone too.

"Envii, just hang up, and I'll talk to Modesty," Goddess begged.

"I'm here. What is going on. I haven't heard from Mina. I tried calling and texting her but got no answer. I went over to Ace's and nobody answered the door. I just thought that Ace was trying to keep her away from me," I replied.

"Ace is in the hospital. Somebody shot him the fuck up, so he ain't with her," Envii spat and started yelling at her kids in the background.

I listened to Envii, Goddess and Kai, but didn't hear anything that I wanted to hear. I flopped down on the couch and Murk sat down next to me. Before I knew it, tears were flowing so fast that I couldn't wipe them if I wanted to. Murk let them know what was going on with me and let them know that he would make some calls. He grabbed me and held me as I cried like I did when Mina was in a coma.

Knock! Knock! Knock!

"Who the fuck is it?" Murk barked.

"Kelly!" My cousin screamed with an attitude.

"I see you still a thief," Murk spat, still holding me as I cried and kissing me on top of my head.

Murk hates my cousin. My cousin is messy as hell and if I gave a fuck about what Murk did, I would have been stopped fucking with him after all the shit that Kelly has told me. Murk didn't move and neither did I. Kelly's ass ain't going nowhere because she wants first dibs on the shit I picked up earlier.

"Will you let her in?" I said as I jumped up and tried to get myself together.

"I won't. That bitch can stand outside until you ready to let her in," Murk spat and made his way out on the patio.

I picked up my phone and tried to call Mina; it rang but she didn't answer. I made my way to my room, picked up some oversized Versace glasses, put them on and made my way to the door as Kelly started calling. I checked myself in the mirror and ran my fingers through my dry ass hair, ignoring Kelly's call. I opened up my style seat app to schedule my appointment with Toya J because unless I'm getting braids, she's the only person that touches my hair.

"I don't know why you still fucking with his ass. He ain't shit and ain't gon' ever be shit. What, that nigga got you in here crying, kicking yo' ass? I never met a bitch that has it all and then some but will let a nigga that can't give you nothing but dick and lies come in and break you down every chance he gets!" Kelly yelled, so Murk could hear her as she looked around for him.

"Bitch, don't get beat the fuck up! What goes on between me and Modesty is me and her business. Worry about yo' baby daddy fucking his homeboy. Ain't no nigga going to no nigga house to watch movies, dumb bitch!" Murk spat as he stood in the patio doorway and shut the door so smoothly like he didn't say what he just did.

Kelly didn't have nothing else to say. Everybody be telling her that nigga Tommy ain't right, but she won't listen. I got Ike on the balcony, and I can't keep my mind off Big Face's disrespectful ass, so I can't offer no advice.

"Come on, ain't no discounts. You can't borrow shit. I don't give a fuck about the party tomorrow. I need all mine," I said, leading the way to the room where I keep my merchandise.

"You just gone let him talk to me like that?" Kelly asked as she slammed the door behind her.

"You know he's not lying. Why you came in here trying to talk shit? You're my cousin, one of the only bitches I fuck with.

What I tell you about my business should be between us. Instead, you bring it up every chance you get. And I know you be telling auntie because my momma knows every damn thing I've ever told you," I said. I flopped down on the lounge that complimented the room like a fancy dressing room.

I even have room dividers that match the room scheme up in two corners for bitches to change. If Ray Ray don't come through like she claims she was, I'm going to the hood and posting up until I get rid of all this shit. Rent is due in a few days, and I'm not asking Murk for shit. I have to cut him off someway because I can't do this anymore. My phone started ringing and when I looked down and saw Big Face's name, I jumped up so damn fast and ran in the bathroom, locking the door behind me.

"Who the fuck chases somebody down in the car when they step foot out the county?" Big Face asked in between laughing.

"The person that made it possible for you to come home. Meanwhile, you thought it was okay for you to be riding with another nigga's bitch," I replied.

"That's the only reason why I called yo ass. I can pay you in dick, I guess. Bitches pay for this, so you ain't getting much. I want some head, but I ain't giving you none and you might get a few pumps."

"Nigga please. I can get that and more from somebody else."

"That's one of the many reason why you could never be my bitch."

"How about you be my bitch?"

Beep, beep, beep.

I know that this nigga didn't hang up on me. I tried to call him back, but he didn't answer. I tried again, and he sent me to voicemail. I texted him and he read it but didn't reply. Now somebody was banging on the bathroom door like the fucking police.

"What?" I said, swinging open the door and it was Murk.

"Get rid of this bitch, so you can ride with me," Murk suggested.

"I got other shit that I need to handle," I said. I walked around him and made my way back to Kelly.

"I know what you said and I got enough for all this, but will you please hold this dress and these heels for me?" Kelly whined.

"Yea... Until another muthafucka hand me some money," I said, taking the money out of her hand and putting the heels and dress back in their proper place.

"Mo, please. I'll give you some weed, and I'll ride with you to Arizona," Kelly begged and caught Murk attention.

"What the fuck are you going to Arizona for?" Murk barked.

"Bye, Kelly. Go and ask Tommy for the money," I suggested and that bitch stomped her way to my kitchen like I did something to her.

"His broke ass ain't got no money, but answer my question, Modesty," Murk threw in.

"Murk, do I question you?" I asked.

"If you going to Arizona for what I think you are, well you know what the fuck it is! Bitch, get the fuck out. You got what you are getting, now go so we can leave!" Murk yelled at Kelly.

"You not gon' keep talking to me crazy like I'm one of yo' bitches because I'm not!" Kelly yelled as she came running out the kitchen

"Bitch, I wouldn't even sit next to you, let alone anything else hoe!" Murk replied.

"Nigga, I'll get somebody to fuck you up!" Kelly said, stepping closer to Murk.

"Bitch, I'll have my niggas snatch up yo' kids and have em' watch me kill you and Tommy gay ass!"

"Stop! What is wrong with y'all?" I said, trying to push Kelly because I damn sure can't push Murk if I tried.

Murk didn't say anything else, but he pulled out his tool

and it pointed towards me and Kelly, since my dumb ass decided to step in the middle of it. I know that Murk won't kill me. This nigga love my dirty panties, but I can't say the same for my cousin. He'll shoot her ass and sit next to me at the funeral like he wasn't the shooter.

6

BIG FACE

"Did you call that damn girl?" My momma questioned.

"Yea, I called her," I replied and finished texting Trina back.

"You better not be fucking lying," My momma nagged.

"When are you going home?" I asked because she is getting on my fucking nerves. I showed her that I called Modesty.

"What the fuck make you think I want to see one of them nasty bitches pussy. Caleb, don't make me hit you upside yo' muthafuckin' head!" My momma spat, swinging on me, but I moved quick enough.

"Damn, my bad. Huh, look, I called the bitch," I said, clicking on the Modesty's name in my messages, begging me to answer her calls.

She should have thought about that before she called me a bitch. I play lots of games, but that ain't one that I play . I don't give a fuck if she did call Iman and get a favor to get me out. I offered the bitch the gifts of my time and dick, and she had to go too damn far. So, her ass can think about the consequences of her actions for a while.

"What do you know about this nigga Sevino?" My momma questioned.

"Shit, not much. I know his people Teflon used to fuck with Envii," I said, rubbing my hands over my face.

"When you supposed to go and meet him?"

"Tomorrow?"

"I don't know about this. Nothing good can come from that girl."

"That girl is your daughter. She not just some bitch off the street. She wouldn't bring no bullshit to us. Regardless of how you feel about her, she loves us. All of us."

"And I love fucking cheesecake, but I can't eat that shit everyday, or I'll be big as a fucking house.

"Momma, I don't know who told you that you was small. You might not be as big as a house, but you damn sure as big as a condo."

"Bri gon' be big as a house before you know it. So, when the fuck do you think that you can take time out of yo' busy schedule to be able to call her?"

"How's OG doing?" I asked, trying to change the subject.

"She's doing good. I went to see her earlier and she asked why you haven't brought yo' big ass up there to see her."

"When they gon' let her come home?"

"They said in a few days as long as they continue to see progress. I need to talk to you about Ace."

"What?" I asked, putting my phone down.

I can tell by the change in her tone that it isn't nothing good.

"He's not doing good. They want us to take him off of life support. Look, I know that it's not easy for you to go to the hospital, but you need to let yo' balls drop and go up there and see him. He would fucking be up there with you!"

"If they want y'all to take him off of life support then that means that he isn't doing good. I can't see him laid up like that. You know I'll do anything for you, for y'all, but that ain't something that I can do."

"That's another reason why you need to talk to Bri. Bri is able to talk to you and get you to—"

"Momma, for real, I don't want to even hear that bitch's name in my house."

"So, what the fuck are you going to do when the baby is born? I'm a whole lot of things, but I ain't no fucking middleman."

"Not a damn thing. What part of that ain't my fucking baby don't you understand? Maybe you need to go and see a damn doctor because I could have sworn we've had this conversation already."

"Fuck you, muthafucka! That is not how I raised you. I don't understand what the fuck you don't understand. I don't give a fuck if Bri fucked fifty niggas. You were still fucking her and the bitch even got a key to this damn house, so how done with her could you really be?"

"It's in her fucking name."

"Yea, keep telling yo'self that's the fucking reason. What are you doing tonight?"

"Not a damn thing, you see this big ass GPS on my ankle. And I'm on fucking curfew. I can't go no damn where until eight. I don't give a damn if I just go to Seven Eleven at eight, I won't be up in this bitch. A nigga feels like I'm still in jail. All for some shit that I didn't do."

"What about the case with that girl?"

"They dropped it. That bitch was lying. I told you that."

"Who's that calling you that you keep sending to voicemail?"

"Damn, ma, is you the damn police?"

"I have to tell you something else."

"Damn, what else?"

"Somebody snatched up Mina and her baby. Gotti and Kurupt came by the hospital today and they want to talk to you."

I PULLED out the driveway in this 2010, black Impala that I bought for Bri back in the day. When she left, she had to leave everything here. And considering my current situation, I need to stay as low key as possible. So, this what the fuck I been driving since I been home. I'm going to meet Kurupt. I don't know what the fuck I'm walking into. This might be a set up, but if I don't go see this nigga, I know he'll come see me, so before I go and meet with Sevino, I'm going to get this over with.

I jumped on the highway and headed downtown. OG called me this morning and we talked for over an hour as she asked me my opinion about what she should do about Ace. She doesn't want him to keep suffering and I get that, but I also don't think she should take him off life support. I have to go and check on Dani and Zay too. That bitch been done turned his damn house into a trap. My momma been going over there to check on her and staying over there some nights, but nobody but Ace has the patience to babysit her ass.

After thirty minutes, I pulled across the street from the Starbucks on Stout and I saw Kurupt's Maybach parked right out front. I scanned the parking lot, but I didn't see anybody or any cars that I recognize. I grabbed Bri's tool that she always kept under the seat and made my way in. I looked around trying to spot Kurupt, but I didn't see him. I walked around and he was at the table all the way in the back. I sat down across from him and he was on the phone with somebody. I checked the time and I still got some time to get across town and meet Sevino.

"I know that my sister was at Ace's house with my niece before she came up missing. I also, know that you were in jail when all this happened. What I don't know is who shot Ace and who y'all been fucking with that would have my sister?" Kurupt asked as soon as he ended his call.

"I don't know who hit Ace if it wasn't y'all. Ain't nobody that would be getting at us," I said as a loud ass nigga in back of me caught my attention.

"Kurupt!" D yelled out like a bitch as he walked up on the table.

Kurupt looked him up and down then at me. I haven't said nothing to this nigga in months. And when I did see him, I didn't have shit to say to him. Him fucking with my money was where I crossed the line. I have a family that is depending on me. My momma hasn't worked in years and nigga, if I don't work, we don't eat. So, worrying about a childhood friend and his bitch problems ain't on my list of things to do.

"I'm in the middle of something ," Kurupt said, catching the white lady across from us attention.

"Bitch, mind ya business," I spat.

The bitch snatched up her coffee and dropped her muffin as she ran away. Muthafuckas need to learn to mind they business. D still ain't ready to hustle. This nigga is a weirdo. He just found a new hoe that ain't trained to chase. Kurupt isn't interested in none of the bullshit that he has to say, so I know that what he thought he had stumbled up on ain't gon' work out in his favor.

"Nigga, that means get the fuck away from my table," Kurupt whispered, but D heard him because he got the fuck on.

"Are you niggas back to hitting licks because y'all ain't bought no product from nobody?" Kurupt asked once D was away from the table.

"We're doing what we have to do," I replied.

"Y'all hitting niggas spots?" Kurupt asked.

"I know what the fuck you trying to get at, but my cousin didn't have shit to do with yo' sister coming up missing. I know you don't fuck with us like that, but my cousin fucks with Mina and he wouldn't let shit happen to her if he could prevent it."

"If I find out different, you won't make it to trial and the rest of your family will be buried next you. Including Brionna and yo' maybe baby," Kurupt said. He put some money on the table and got up to leave.

~

"Shnikia, shut the fuck up or take yo' ass to the car," Sevino said as I walked up on him and this girl at the Cherry Creek Reservoir.

"You shut the fuck up. I'm not going no fucking where," The bitch replied.

"Big Face?" Sevino asked once I got up by them.

"Yup," I said as we shook up.

"How do you know this nigga? He on fucking GPS and yo' stupid ass want to meet up with him. When yo' dumb ass be in jail, maybe this nigga will write you and come see you because I'm not!" The bitch yelled and walked away.

My momma was right, my sister is definitely a hoe. That is definitely that nigga's bitch and this nigga got my sister calling him daddy. When she call me later on, I'm gon' cuss her ass out.

"My girl doesn't know how to act. But she do got a point, nigga, you is hot as hell," Sevino said as soon as his girl was far enough away.

"I'm good. This ain't stopping shit," I assured him.

If I have to get to it from nine to five then that's what it is. But if he was really connected as Nia claims, we can both benefit from this. We walked the trail and talked business for about twenty minutes, then his bitch started honking the horn.

"Just ignore her. She a lil slow," Sevino suggested.

I thought my bitches didn't know how to act. They at least know when I'm handling business not to get on my damn nerves, but this bitch here doesn't give a fuck. If this nigga can't handle his bitch, that says a lot about how he might handle business.

"Nia is the home girl and she solid, so I'm willing to fuck with you on the strength of her. We also have some of the same enemies."

I know he was referring to Kurupt and his people. They trippin' over a bitch, but the shit we got going on between us is way deeper than that. We finished talking while I weighed my options. I don't have time to be used as pawn for these niggas to be trying to get back at Kurupt and his people. I got my own fucking problems. We walked the trail a little longer and finally made it back to where we were parked at. His phone was ringing nonstop, and I know it was his bitch calling.

"I know her ass didn't leave me out here," Sevino spat.

I made my way back to the car as Sevino and his bitch argued over the phone. I got my own damn problems. As I pulled the handle to the door, my phone started ringing and it was Mo, but I sent her ass to voicemail. As soon as I did that, my phone started ringing and it was Brionna calling me on Facetime.

"What Brionna?" I answered, pulling off as Sevino's bitch pulled up.

7

MODESTY

"Why couldn't I just give you yo' key back?" I asked Murk as we rode to his storage.

"Because were not done. I don't give a fuck what you talking about," Murk insisted as he weaved in and out of traffic.

I tried to talk to him, but that got me nowhere. He can think whatever the fuck he wants to think, that's on him. I told him what it was and that it was never going to work, so we needed to just go our separate ways. Shit, I even offered for us to still be friends and that wasn't good enough for him.

We pulled up to the storage and he jumped out. I tried to call Big Face again and if he doesn't answer this time, I'm done trying to call or text his ass. I don't even know why I'm tripping about his ass. I just don't understand how you can be with a muthafucka everyday, and then for no reason start acting funny with me like I did something to him. He so damn childish ignoring me.

"Why the fuck haven't you been answering my calls?" I asked as soon as the call connected.

"What's up Mo?" Big Face asked like I he didn't hear my question.

"What did I do to you to have you ignoring my calls."

"I got a lot of shit going on right now and to be honest, I don't feel like talking to nobody."

"What are you doing?" I asked because I wanted to see him.

"Why, you want me to do you?"

"Nigga, no."

"Whatever. Not shit, at the house."

"Um, nigga, you not gon' ask me what I'm doing?"

"Modesty, I don't give a fuck what are you doing. If you want to slide, you can, I'm at the house. If not, I'll see you when I see you," Big Face said and ended the call.

Murk came back to his truck carrying two duffle bags. He kept some of his money here, so I guess that's what's in the bags. Murk popped the trunk, threw the bags in and then disappeared again. What the fuck is he doing? That is exactly why I didn't want to come. When he hands me the key back, I'm going to put in the door panel, that way we won't have no reason to talk to each other after that. I know that it isn't going to be that easy, but I'll deal with it as it comes.

My phone started ringing and it was my momma. I haven't talked to her since I moved out her house. I know her and Gotti been talking big shit because that is what they do. I do miss my nieces and nephew, but fuck Gotti. He think he's my fucking dad and that's the problem.

"Hey, momma," I said as I answered the phone.

"What the fuck is yo' problem? What type of daughter don't even come and see they momma? Even Gotti ain't been over here, but I guess you too good to come and check on me. Y'all muthafuckas are going to miss me when I'm gone," my momma nagged.

"I'll be by tomorrow to see you."

"What if I wake up dead tomorrow?" My momma whined.

"Momma," I replied as Murk got back into the truck.

"What's up, momma?" Murk said as he started the truck.

"Who is that? Is that Murk? He the only one that been over here to check on me," she bragged.

"Alright, momma, I'll see you tomorrow," I said and rushed her ass off the phone.

"Why are you going to my momma's?" I asked, irritated because I think I know why the fuck he would be going over there.

"Because she called me."

"Stop playing with me, Murk. Called you for what?"

"You know what she called me for, Modesty."

"I'm 'bout to go pick up some work and take it to yo' crack-head momma then take Nanny drunk ass a bottle and see how the fuck you like t—" I said.

Murk grabbed me by my neck, banged my head into the dashboard and then into the passenger side window. I closed my eyes and opened them back up, but I couln't see clear. Then everything faded black.

"Wake the fuck up! The police are behind us," Murk barked.

I squinted my eyes because the lights from the cars were making me even more dizzy than I already am. Running my hands through my hair, I struggled to keep my eyes open. My head was throbbing, and I felt like the car was spinning. Just when I thought that it couldn't get any worse, an officer walked up to the passenger side window with a fucking flashlight on me.

"Can I see your license and registration?" The officer on his side asked.

"Ma'am, are you okay?" The officer asked as he moved the flashlight, so it wasn't shining directly on me.

"Yea, she's okay. She got a headache," Murk answered for me.

"I wasn't talking to you, buddy," he officer replied.

"Ma'am, what's your name?" The officer asked.

"Modesty Williams," I managed to say and then the officer disappeared.

"What the fuck are they talking about?" Murk asked like I knew the fucking answer.

"Ma'am, please step out of the car," the officer requested.

"Excuse me, for what? I'm not stepping out of shit," I replied.

"Ma'am, there is a warrant out for your arrest. So, I'm going to ask you again to please step out of the vehicle.

"A warrant for what?" I questioned as I got out of the truck.

"For the possession or sale of stolen items," The officer said as he swiftly cuffed me.

⁓

"Why won't you just come home, Modesty?" Goddess asked as we walked out of the jail.

"I'm not coming home, G," I said as I got in her truck.

"I don't understand why—"

"I ain't trying to cut you off, but I need you to hurry up and get out of this parking lot," I requested, not wanting to see Murk.

"Just come to the house for tonight. The kids miss you," Goddess suggested.

"I'll come over tomorrow," I said, texting Big Face to see if he's still up.

"Why? Who are you trying to go see and are you going to tell me why you were arrested?"

"It's nothing, I'll handle it."

"Listen, I know that I've said it a million times and you're sick of hearing me say it, but Gotti does miss you, and he wants what's best for you. I hate to say it, but this right here is not what he wants for you. He busts his ass to provide for his family," Goddess said, defending Gotti being an asshole.

"He sells drugs, you act like that nigga is a respectable citizen. G, thank you for coming to get me and here's your money, but I don't want to talk about Gotti. Matter fact, you can let me out right here," I said, tired of hearing her mouth and putting the five hundred dollars in her cup holder.

"No, I'm not letting you out on this corner, Modesty. Okay, I'll just shut up," Goddess offered.

"Why hasn't Gotti been to see momma?" I asked.

"I don't know."

I know that she's lying because that nigga tells her every damn thing. She just wants me to talk to Gotti, but I'm not. I only called her because I was trying to get rid of Murk and unfortunately, a bitch had to go to jail for that to happen. I'm not going home because I'm sure the nigga is lurking nearby trying to see if I'm home.

"Who lives over here?" Goddess's nosy ass asked.

"My friend," I replied.

"Your friend who?"

"Thanks, G, I'll call you before I come over tomorrow," I said, jumping out her truck before she could completely stop.

I forgot how nosy she was. Damn, her and all her damn questions, she was worse than the police. I turned around and G was still sitting out here waiting for me to get in the house. I waved at her as the door opened. I rushed in, so she couldn't see Big Face.

"What the fuck were you in jail for?" Big Face questioned as I lead the way through his house.

"Long story," I replied as I plopped down on the couch.

"Take anything out this bitch, I'll snap yo fucking neck," Big Face seriously responded.

"Shut up, you won't even hit a female," I said, rolling my eyes then snatching the remote and changing the channel.

I don't want to watch the Animal channel. His phone started ringing, but he didn't answer it which surprised me. He always answers his phone. He doesn't give a fuck who it is either. I turned on Orange is the New Black and his phone started ringing again, but this time, he didn't even look to see who it was.

"Why you didn't answer yo' phone?" I asked once it stopped ringing.

"Mo, don't start questioning me and shit," Big Face spat.

I didn't respond because he'll just keep on going and won't shut up about it if I say something.

"Why yo' hair ain't combed and why your nails look like that?"

"You want to get my hair and nails done?" I asked, not taking my eyes off the TV as Big Face ran his fingers through my hair.

"Yea, maybe... maybe fucking not. You been smoking?" Big face said and pushed my hair in my face.

"Did you fuck Bri?" I asked, knowing I didn't want to know the answer, but I had to ask.

"Not today."

I jumped up before he could finish responding. What the fuck is that supposed to mean. Did you fuck the bitch yesterday or the day before?

"Where the fuck is you going?" Big Face yelled out. I made my way to the bathroom to get in the shower.

I turned on the shower and jumped in. I heard Big Face screaming my name, but I just kept ignoring him. I've been over here a bunch of times and I was surprised that my stuff was still here and a bitch ain't took it or been using my shit. Everything is right where I left it. I know some bitches been over here, but he'll never tell me that.

"What the fuck?" I said as I grabbed my towel and got out the shower. Big Face was sitting on the toilet.

"Did you hear me calling yo' name?" He asked.

"Yea, but just like you didn't have to answer me, I don't have to answer you."

"What you get in shower for? You ain't staying here? Slide means slide in and slide out."

"Because I just got out of jail."

"You just got out of jail? You were in there for a few hours. Girl, ain't nobody make any free you post on Facebook. Girl, you weren't in jail."

I rolled my eyes and looked over at Big Face. He was giving me a look that he has given me many times, but we never went there. I made my way out the bathroom and down the hallway to his room. I went to his dresser and got one of his t-shirts. I made my way downstairs, to put my clothes in the washer. Big Face was back on the couch watching TV. My phone started ringing and it was Murk.

"Cook something," Big Face suggested.

I made my way to the kitchen to find something to cook. I looked up and Big Face was sitting at the island on one of the bar stools watching me. I know what he likes, so I decided to make some pork chops, green beans and rice-a-roni. This nigga is so damn hood. Every move I made, he was watching me.

"You know how to cook. Why couldn't you cook for me?" I asked.

"Women are supposed to cook. Ain't you a woman?"

"Whatever nigga."

"So, what is going on with you and yo' niggas?"

"I cut them all off," I admitted.

"For me?"

"No, not for you."

It was time for me to let Murk go and the others weren't playing they roles because they all in their feelings, so I have been cutting them off slowly. Murk isn't just going to walk away. When Murk said that we weren't done, he really believes that. We do have history, but I can't keep doing what I've been doing with him.

"I'm gon' be real with you. I'm not gon' be yo' man. I'm not paying yo' bills or keeping you."

"I never have asked you to be my man or take care of me. But you be acting like you don't fuck with me at all. Nigga, I was with you when you got arrested and before that, I was with yo' ass damn near every day."

"See, that's what I'm talking about. Yea, you cool and we were kicking it, but that's just what it was. Me and you wouldn't work. You a thief. Why you think I came to the bathroom to watch you? It damn sure wasn't to see that lil pussy."

"Are you serious?"

"Nigga, you met my brother trying to steal his car. I like my bitches in the house. I don't want a bitch out there in the streets. You be posted up in the spots and all types of shit. Not my bitch," Big Face said, shaking his head.

"You like yo' bitches in the house huh? I'm a lil confused because I know a few of yo' bitches and none of them be sitting in the damn house cooking and cleaning. They be all of in the mix. Red is a rat, Bri can make you any type of paperwork that you need. And don't let me get started on Trina's rat ass."

"Brionna was my bitch, but the other ones wasn't, and I'm not gon' discuss Brionna with you."

I know that he fucked with Bri for years. And I know they probably still fucking but she has a whole nigga. I'm just confused on why he is so protective when it comes to her. Why is she so special? Why won't he just let her go? The nigga looks at me crazy whenever I even bring her up. I finished cooking because I was not going to get anywhere with this conversation.

"Where my plate at?" Big Face asked as I walked by him with mine.

"In the fucking cabinet," I said and made my to the living room.

"What type of woman don't fix a man's plate?" Big Face yelled.

"The type of woman that you would never be her man!"

We sat in the living room and watched tv for a few hours. Big Face talked shit about any and every damn thing. All he does is talk shit, I got up because I couldn't fight it anymore. I was tired as fuck and needed to get some sleep. The way things have been going I know that I have a long day ahead of me.

"Where the fuck is you going?" Big Face asked.

"To bed," I said and kept on walking.

I've slept in his bed before, so I don't know why he is acting surprised. I could hear him downstairs doing something, but I don't know what and don't care. I got in his bed and just stared at the ceiling. I picked up my phone off the nightstand, went to my favorites and pushed Mina's name. I just got Mina back and already she's gone again. I heard Big Face yelling at somebody. Just like I figured, Mina's phone just rang, I didn't get an answer.

With the life our brothers live, anybody could have snatched Mina. From a nigga that was mad because they wouldn't put them on to any nigga that's just mad and hating. When I was younger, I hated the fact that my brother was always so protective over me. I couldn't do anything but go to Mina's. Even then he was always calling and just popping up.

"Don't be calling yo' niggas while you laying in my bed to tell them goodnight," Big Face spat as he flopped down on the bed.

"That's you yelling at bitches. Which one was that?"

"None of yo' damn business," Big Face spat, snatching the covers like it wasn't an icebox in this damn house.

"Um, I'm cold too," I said and attempted to snatch the cover back but got nowhere because he was holding on too tight.

"Aww, you want me to hold you?"

I thought about it and after the past few days I've had, that would be nice. Just as I snuggled up to him and put my leg on him, he started talking shit. I didn't care, it's cold. Being this close to him, I can get some of the fucking cover that he is trying to hog.

"You got to go in the morning when I wake up," Big Face said, catching me off guard.

I didn't respond. I'm not the type that is going to beg him to be around me. If I have to go in the morning, that's what it is. I'm not about to ask no questions or nothing because the facts still remain the same, I know Big Face talks a lot of shit. He said that he would never be with me and I have to accept that.

"You better not cut me again or slice up my sheets with them long ass toe nails!" Big Face yelled.

"Shut up. Why do you always have to be so loud?"

"Because I can," Big Face said as he scooted so close to me, I could feel his breath.

As Big Face stared at me, I started feeling uncomfortable because he wasn't saying anything, just staring. Big Face learned a little closer and kissed me. As many times as I wanted to kiss him, this has never happened before and it feels right. As his hands started roam all over my body, I instantly got chills and got nervous.

"Are you good? You're shaking and shit?" Big Face questioned, taking a break from our kiss.

"Yea," I replied, still slightly trembling.

I kissed him, trying to not make this as awkward as this is becoming. He slipped two fingers into my pussy that was now dripping and did not miss a beat as I started to grind on his fingers. I just hoped that he kissed my pussy the way that he was kissing me. Big Face rolled over on me and started doing something on the nightstand, but not breaking our kiss.

He broke our kiss and got up off the bed. I felt myself still shaking, so I had to have a fucking quick talk with myself because I don't know what the fuck is going on with me. I've never been like this before with any nigga. I don't know what it is about this nigga that has me feeling like this. I've been with niggas with more money and status than him, and I've been with niggas that were beneath him, but none of them ever made me feel like he does. All of them kissed my ass and begged for my time and attention. Meanwhile, this nigga wouldn't beg me for a muthafucking thing. It's something about that, that makes me want to be around him as much as I can.

Looking over at Big Face, he was putting on a condom and snatched the lil bit of clothing I had on off of me. He pulled me to the edge of the bed, stepping in between my legs and eased his long, thick dick inside of me slowly. He started off slow stroking and then picked up the speed, the whole time never taking his eyes off of me. Big Face grabbed onto my hips and started pushing inside of me even faster, but now harder, making me scream out. I wanted to scream out, but my words were stuck in my throat.

"Fucckkk, yo' pussy kinda straight," Big Face said as a smirk spread across his face.

I know that I'm making some ugly ass faces and I can tell by the way he was looking at me, but shit, I couldn't help it. His dick was good as hell. My pussy was kind of straight, yea fucking right, all the sounds this nigga is making. He pulled my right leg, putting it on his left shoulder, but not before he stuck three of my toes in his mouth and sucked on them.

"Glad yo' fucking feet ain't dirty," Big Face said, causing both of us to laugh.

"Shut the fuck up," I replied, still laughing.

He pulled out of me and tapped me on the leg, telling me to roll over. I rolled over, spreading my legs and arching my back. Before I could even brace myself, Big Face was back inside of me. I was screaming his name so loud that if his neighbors didn't know his name, they damn sure know it now. I couldn't help it, it felt so fucking good. And when he slapped me on my ass, it just made it even better.

"What are you doing?" Big Face asked as he took two of his fingers and rubbed my clit, not slowing up on the back shots.

8

AHMINA

"Why won't she stop crying?" Tycoon asked as he paced the room with Tiana.

"She doesn't know you," I said, finally breaking the silent treatment that I had been giving him since them dumb niggas snatched me and Tiana up five days ago.

"She does know me. I'm her dad. What the fuck are you talking about?" Tycoon questioned with an attitude.

"Whatever," I said and rolled my chair back over to the TV.

"Mina, I can't believe you're acting like this. All the times that we used to talk about being back together and raising our daughter, having the family that neither one of us ever had."

"Please, get out of my face."

"Why did you leave Kurupt's?"

Tycoon finally gave up trying to get Tiana to stop crying and handed her to me. He lasted longer than I thought that he would. I'm so sick of him asking me about Kurupt like he really gives a fuck. He can't do anything for me. The only thing he can do is drop me off at Mo's. He took my phone and won't give it back. And I know by now that Mo and Kai are worried.

"How did you get out early?" I asked.

"I told you, I paroled early."

"Then why when I looked online it said your earliest release date was years from now?"

"Shit, I don't know. What, you want a nigga to be locked up? You don't want me to be out here, so that I can provide for you and my daughter?"

I rolled my eyes and didn't say anything. The last thing I need is to get me and Tiana caught up in any of Tycoon's shit. Nobody has hurt me the way that Tycoon did. I used to want to be with him, but those days are gone. I'm not interested in being anything with him. The fact that he would think that kidnapping us was the way to get his family back is crazy as hell to me. I'm in so much pain because I don't have my meds and this nigga think he can just go and get random pain pills off the street, and I'm going to take them.

"You're clearly in pain. You need to take some of these fucking pills!" Tycoon yelled.

"Who the fuck do you think I am, one of them rat hoes you be fucking with? I don't take pills that weren't prescribed to me, dumb ass!"

"I can't do nothing for yo' ungrateful ass! Nothing is never good enough for you!"

"Thanks for kidnapping us. How could I ever repay you?" I asked as some weird ass nigga came in the room.

"Mina, could you give me a minute, so I can holla at my man Dro?" Tycoon's slow ass asked.

"Muthafucka, I can't walk!" I screamed as loud as I could.

He didn't waste his time saying anything. He made his way out of the room with Dro following close behind. I've seen that weird ass nigga before. I don't know where I saw him, but I definitely have seen him somewhere. Why couldn't this nigga go and kidnap Jess and her daughter? Well, maybe Ace's daughter. Whoever fucking daughter she is. He could have went and got them and just left me and my daughter the fuck alone. I feel so fucking hopeless. Tiana keeps looking at me. I know that she doesn't know what's going on, but I damn sure feel bad for putting her through any of this. She doesn't deserve this. If Tycoon was any type of man, he wouldn't do this to us.

Knock, knock, knock.

I don't know who the fuck it is but I'm not about to answer the door. This ain't my fucking house. I don't even know where the fuck we're at. All I know is weird ass niggas keep coming in and out of here. He's the black sheep in his family, so I'm not surprised I haven't seen any of them. Not one of these niggas have said welcome home. So, who knows who these weirdos are.

"You hungry?" Tycoon asked.

"I need to call my doctor, so he can call me in a new subscription."

"Huh, put it on speaker."

"You think I know his number by heart? Are you fucking dumb? I need my phone, dumb ass!"

Tycoon stormed out the room and came back with my phone fully charged. I already know that he's been looking through my phone. I went through my contacts and found the doctors number with Tycoon breathing down my neck, reeking of cigarettes and cheap ass liquor. As I pressed call, he snatched the phone out of my hand ,put it on speaker and stood in front of me with the phone.

"You really are a bitch!" I yelled.

Tycoon hit me so hard, me and Tiana damn near hit the floor. The only thing that stopped us was me grabbing the end table as the doctor answered the phone. Tiana started screaming so loud that my ears started to ring.

"Hello, hello," Dr, Desai repeatedly said as Tycoon just stared at me, damn near foaming at the mouth.

"Yea, my girl need you to call in her prescription," Tycoon managed to say not taking his eyes off of me.

"And who is your girl, sir?" Dr. Desabi asked.

"Ahmina, Ahmina Wright," Tycoon spat.

"Can I speak to Ms. Wright?"

"Hello," I said, rocking Tiana trying to get her to calm down.

"Ms. Wright, I have been trying to contact you. In order for you to have a chance on recovering it is important that you are meeting with the therapist and completing physical therapy as I recommended. My team has been trying to contact you and your brother. Is there something going on?" Dr. Desabi asked.

"No, ain't shit wrong, she just needs her

fucking prescription called in!" Tycoon screamed.

"Ms. Wright, I can have one of my nurses bring your medication to you, but what is your plan with the physical therapy?"

"I'll have to get back to you about tha—"

"You're a real doctor, right? So, just call the prescription in. I'll tell you where to call it in to," Tycoon demanded and walked out of the room.

Why the fuck can't the nurse come here? This nigga is moving real strange and I don't know what the fuck is going on with him. I need to figure out how to get me and my daughter the fuck out of here. I know Kai done told my brother by now and I know he's looking for me. Why the fuck hasn't he found me? Where the fuck is Ace, shit, Envii and everybody fucking else? Why hasn't anybody found us?

"Come the fuck on, you have to go with me because of the type of fucking medicine yo' stupid ass has to take," Tycoon spat as he came storming into the room.

"I'm stupid?" I questioned.

"Yes, you're fucking stupid. You was fucking with that worker ass nigga, running from that bum ass nigga and got hit by a fucking car. You're fucking stupid. I don't know why I ever fucked with you let alone had a baby with you! And shut her the fuck up, I'm sick of hearing her fucking cry! Be a fucking mother and do yo' fucking job!" Tycoon spat and made his way out the house, slamming the door behind him. Dro came back to the room to help me and Tiana out the house.

"Kurupt, is your brother?" Dro asked.

"Yea," I mumbled.

"How you end up fucking with him?" Dro whispered. I didn't respond, and he kept pushing my chair to the all-black, Yukon Denali.

"Put her ass all the way in the back!" Tycoon ordered.

"I'll give you a hundred thousand if you help me," I propositioned Dro.

His eyes bulged out of his head, but he didn't respond. I know he not no real getting money nigga. I know that he wants the money and probably needs the fucking money. Tycoon started the truck and turned up the music so loud that the windows started shaking. Dro got us into the truck, looked around and kickout one of the back headlights. Tycoon didn't even hear it. Dro mouthed, *I got you* to me and closed the back of the truck. All I could do is wait to see if he's going to do anything.

As we rode, I looked around trying to see if I could figure out where the fuck we were at. I offered Dro all that I had in this world. If he can get me and Tiana the fuck away from this nigga, he can have it all. It's all the money that Tycoon's family has ever given me since Tiana was born. I never needed to spend none of it. I'm willing to lose it all to get me and my baby away from this nigga.

I saw lights flashing and this nigga was still driving like a bat out of hell. As they get closer and all the other cars pulled over, this dumb ass nigga was still driving. When I looked back, I saw that they were behind us and it's the police pulling us over. Never in my life have I been so happy to see the police.

"Pull over now!" One of the officers ordered from behind us.

Dro was arguing with Tycoon. I couldn't hear what they were saying, but Dro is definitely mad. Tycoon pulled over and turned the music down. He looked back at me in the rearview mirror with hate in his eyes.

"Kill the engine and throw the keys out the window," the police ordered. Tycoon hesitated but he followed the instructions.

"Nigga, what the fuck is wrong with you?" Dro barked.

"Nigga, you act like you know who the fuck I am?" Tycoon questioned.

"Muthafucka, yo' seed is in this car and yo' girl. Nigga, you out yo' fucking body!" Dro replied.

"Nigga, you don't worry about them. That's my fucking business! Just do yo' fucking job!" Tycoon demanded.

"Driver, exit the vehicle slowly!" An officer requested.

What the fuck is taking so long, get this nigga. Take his ass back to jail and get us the fuck out of this truck. It feels like everything is going is slow motion. Why the fuck are they giving out orders minutes apart. And this nigga is moving at his own speed. He ain't in no rush to get out of the truck. He is pissing me off, so hopefully the police feeling the same fucking way and off this nigga's head. When he got out and I didn't hear shots, I couldn't help but to be disappointed, but in all relieved because there is no way that he is getting back in this truck.

"Y'all good?" Dro asked.

"Yea, we good," I replied.

"Why the fuck them bitches ain't came to the truck yet and that nigga ain't in cuffs?" Dro questioned.

I turned around and I can't really see anything because it's dark outside and the headlights on the now three cop cars are now damn near blinding me, so I turned back around. I don't know how Tiana is sleeping through any of this. I guess she got tired and finally cried herself to sleep. I promise myself whatever the fuck I have to do, I am going to get my daughter the fuck away from this nigga, and he will never get close to us again.

"Can I see your phone?" I asked.

"Here this nigga come," Dro replied.

"Text 720-358-1172. Text the address to the house where I've been at," I said as I looked back. Tycoon was walking like it wasn't shit back to the truck and the officers were speeding off.

"I got you," Dro ensured me.

"Ahmina, you kicked the fucking headlight and nigga, you let the bitch do it?" Tycoon questioned as he got back in the truck.

"How the fuck did you get to drive away?" Dro asked.

"Nigga, my name holds weight," Tycoon boasted.

"Naw, nigga, yo' momma and em' name hold weight. They don't even fuck with you," Dro replied.

I didn't say shit because I won't ever say nothing to this bitch ass nigga ever again in my life if I can help it. I thought that he had done the worst that he could do to me with the bitches and baby, but that pain isn't shit compared to the pain that I have been feeling for the past five days. Ever since them niggas brought me to that house, I knew that shit was going to get worse and sure enough, it has. I don't know why I had faith that the police could do anything for me because they damn sure didn't even come to check on us. I'm so confused. I know this nigga doesn't have a license. Why? I don't know, but he doesn't. They still let this nigga drive off. They must be on his momma's payroll.

We pulled up to a Walgreens and Tycoon threw the truck into park as he parked in the middle of two parking spots.

Dro jumped out and started to help me and Tiana out the truck because I damn sure wasn't leaving my daughter in the truck with this nigga. Dro got us out the truck and Tycoon called out to Dro.

"Nigga, no more talking on my fuckin' talking to my bitch!" Tycoon called out.

"I don't who the fuck you think you talking too, nigga, but you not about to keep talking to me like I'm yo' bitch!" Dro barked, walking back over to the truck.

I rolled myself into the store to get my medicine because I don't give a fuck about Dro or Tycoon. I should have stayed my ass at Kurupt's, I'm sure my electric chair was delivered by now. Here I am struggling to get down the aisles. This white lady brushed past me, looking at me crazy like I didn't belong here. After the ride here, I damn sure don't know where we are at. I can tell by the people that are in this Walgreens that they damn sure don't want my black ass in here.

Pop! Pop! Pop! Rat-a- tat- tat.

As I waited in line for my medicine, all I could hear was gun shots and white people screaming. The pharmacy tech and the pharmacist both hit the floor screaming bloody murder because of the shooting outside. I turned around and saw masked man swarming the pharmacy and running in my direction. As tears started to run down my face, the masked men got closer and closer. As bad as I wanted to run away, there is no way that I could in my current state. All I can do is pray that my brother is coming for us.

9

BIG FACE

"What's up, Brionna?" I said as I opened my eyes.

She was standing at the foot of my bed with her scarf still on. She looked like she ain't washed her face or brushed her teeth, let alone her ass, but here she is to argue bright and fucking early. Looking at the clock, it's seven o'clock and here she is just looking at me but hasn't said shit. I guess I'm supposed to guess what the fuck her problem is today. I haven't talked to Bri since the day I got of jail, but I can tell you what the bitch ate for breakfast yesterday because she calls my momma a hundred times a day like she her momma. I wouldn't call her momma either, so I don't give a fuck about her talking to momma.

"Why the fuck you ain't been answering my calls?" Bri finally asked as I sat up and leaned against my headboard.

"We don't have shit to discuss. Right now, my only concern is my family. As you know, I got a lot of shit going on. I can't be worried about yo' fucking problems, that's what you got a nigga for. He should be able to make sure you good. That's why you with him, right?"

"We don't have nothing to discuss? Are you fucking serious?

I'm carrying your fucking child, we have a lot to fucking discuss! What you're not about to do is just say fuck me and leave me and your child and walk away! What the fuck did I do to you to deserve this? After all that you've put me through! All the shit that I've done for you, and this is how you trying to do me!"

"Brionna, you left. I didn't leave you. When you left, that was it. I ain't gon' lie, it was hard to walk away and that is why I still kept you so close. I loved yo' ass. I busted my ass to make sure that you were good and that wasn't good enough for you. So, I don't want to hear none of that shit you talking about. You can get the fuck on and leave my fucking keys on the table downstairs," I said as I picked up my ringing phone.

"Hello," I said, answering Nia's call.

Brionna plopped down on my bed like she didn't hear what the fuck I just said. As I waited for the call to connect, I just looked at Brionna because now she's staring all in my face. I know that I fucked up when I kept fucking Brionna after she left. Where it didn't mean shit to me, it made her think that one day that we would be back together and I'd give her what she begged a nigga for.

"Why haven't you got back with him?" Nia questioned as soon as the call connected.

"I'm trying to figure shit out. Nia, I'm not jumping to do shit right now," I admitted.

"Nigga, I know that you fucked up by what is going on with Ace, but you have to keep on living. He is going to come out of this and walk up out of there. In the meantime, you need to step up and handle business, so he has something to come home to. This nigga is offering you whatever that you need on the strength of me. Let yo' balls drop, nigga, and get this money!" Nia replied.

"Fuck you, my shit is hanging!"

"Why the fuck is you doing my girl like that? You know that

when it all falls down, she is the only girl other than momma that really gives a fuck about you," Nia nagged.

"I ain't doing shit to yo' girl, she did this shit to herself. I'm not taking care of no baby that ain't fucking mi—" I attempted to say as Bri leaped across the bed and jumped on me.

"I fucking hate you! How the fuck could you say some shit like that!" Bri yelled as she swung on me. I pushed her off of me and jumped off the bed.

"Keep, yo' fucking hands off me. I already told you to get the fuck out. I don't know why the fuck you're still here. I've put you through so much and did you so wrong and yo' ass still keep coming back. Make it make sense, Brionna. Move the fuck on and let a nigga go. Go and live happily ever after with that other nigga. You think you about to come over here and fight me because that nigga over there kicking yo' ass, you got me fucked up. The only thing that is saving yo' ass is I don't put my hands on bitch—"

"You need to fucking leave!" Nia yelled in my ear.

"I'm not leaving shit. This is my fucking house. I pay the bills here. This bitch need to leave."

"It's in her fucking name. Did you forget that?"

"So fucking what? It's been in her fucking name, and I still ain't going no fucking where. Nia, stay out of my fucking business."

"How is OG doing?" Nia asked as Bri just sat on my bed crying in her hands.

I walked away because I'm sick of looking at her and made my way to the bathroom. I finished talking to Nia and told her that I would call that nigga . Bri do all this shit and then cry and whine like I'm the fucking problem. I haven't done shit to her ass, but it's always my fault. Then I have to listen to my momma about why we need to be together. Bri thought that if she went out and fuck with another nigga it would make me mad and we would get back together. She right about one thing, it made me mad as hell because of how the fuck she went about it. She went behind my back and was fucking that nigga for who knows how long. Shit, I was hardly ever home and when I was, she wasn't. She would tell me she was with her sisters or home girls and come to find out, she was with that nigga. One day she got mad because she had been home for three days, and I finally came home. She just blurted it out that she was fucking Bad News.

"Open the fucking door!" Bri yelled, banging on the bathroom door.

I ended the call with Nia and turned on the shower, then brushed my teeth like I didn't hear her crazy ass banging on the door like a maniac. I don't know what the fuck she could want, but I damn sure don't have shit else to say. Checking the time on my phone, I know that she has to leave soon to meet her nigga, so eventually she'll run her ass out of here.

Starting up the car and backing out the driveway, I saw a black Yukon Denali parked across the street with windows tinted so dark I can't see who's in it, but I know that it's not none of my neighbors' cars. My phone started ringing, but I didn't even look down at it. My eyes were in the rearview mirror looking at the Denali. Whoever the fuck it is cranked their ignition and Meek Mills blared from their truck, causing their trunk to rattle and they skirted off. Bri been gone a few hours and I know it ain't Bad News. I thought about who it could have been as I watched them go down the street until they disappeared. It could have been one of Kurupt's niggas, but they would have said or done something. He doesn't have the type of niggas around him that don't make shit shake. He only has niggas around him that will put in work.

I called my momma back as I pulled away from the house.

"Where are you at?" My momma yelled as she answered the phone.

"Leaving the house. What's up?"

"You need to get up to the hospital now!" My momma demanded.

"Momma, you know how I feel about the fucking hospital. I done told you I can't come up to the fucking hospi—"

"Listen, muthafucka, somebody broke into Ace's house and...," my momma said and blew into the phone.

"And what?" I yelled as the phone beeped letting me know that the phone disconnected.

10

MODESTY

"Auntie, where is Kelly?" I asked as I walked in her front door.

"I don't know, but don't walk in my house and not speak to everybody," My aunt Lish insisted.

"Hi, everybody," I replied, rolling my eyes at this nigga that she just can't seem to let go.

My momma was addicted to crack and my auntie drug of choice is this nigga. No matter what he does to her or her kids, she doesn't give a fuck. She is never going to leave this nigga alone. If anybody says anything to her about this nigga, she is willing to go toe to toe about his sorry ass.

"When was the last time you seen her?" I asked, looking around because I know my auntie and I know she be fucking lying.

"How the fuck you get out of jail? Who you tell on?" Claud, my aunt's man asked.

"Tell Kelly that I'm looking for her," I told my auntie, but still looking at Claud.

I turned to walk away and before I could reach to open the door, I heard Kelly's voice from behind me. I turned back around and ran towards that bitch. I know that she was the one that talked to the police about me and if it wasn't her, it was damn sure her sister or somebody that she told. She was the only one that had been to my fucking house. I can't say that I'm surprised.

As I pounced on Kelly's ass and banged her head into the dirty ass hardwood floors, I could hear my brother telling me, *"Them bitches don't like you. They are jealous of you. They mad because you ain't in the fucking hood with them."* They always wanted to borrow something, hold a few dollars and my dumb ass was always hollering they my cousins and this and that, but my brother was right all along.

"Get the fuck off my daughter. Claud, get that bitch!" Lisha yelled out.

"Muthafucka, if you touch me, my brother will kill yo' whole fucking family!" I yelled out as I pinned Kelly's arms down with my thighs.

Each time my fist connected with her face, I wanted her to never forget this. As her nose and mouth started to bleed out and blood started to splatter all over my tank top, I glanced back over my shoulder and now Claud and Lisha were arguing. I would never call Gotti about this, but they didn't know that. Lisha was more scared of Gotti than Claud was, but he knew better. My brother done kicked his ass on several occasions for him beating on Lisha and Lisha was mad at Gotti because Claud left.

Kelly wanted to be me so bad and even with Murk. She talked all that shit about Murk, but I saw messages on her messenger that she had tried on several occasion to try to get with Murk. I never said anything because I didn't really care. She wanted some shit that she would never have and that wasn't my fault or problem. When I was satisfied and out of breath, I got off of Kelly and as Lisha rushed over, I knocked her right on her ass.

"Fuck you, bitch! All that I did for you and yo' brother and this is how you do me?" Lisha yelled out.

"Yea, and you let Claud molest me and yo' daughters. You're a miserable old hoe!" I yelled as I walked past Claud and hit him across his face with my tool.

When you turn sixteen, most girls get a car. Gotti, bought me a gun and took me to the shooting range before we went to my birthday dinner. He always told me that he wouldn't always be there to protect me, and I needed to learn how to protect myself. Goddess was against that and knowing her past, I never understood why she thought like she did, but I respect that she just wasn't about that life. I made my way to my truck and as I went to pull out, the police pulled behind me, blocking me in. As I got out of my truck, I saw Goddess and Envii running towards me.

"What the fuck is going on?" Envii asked as the police officers got of their car.

"Ma'am, are you Modesty?" One of the officers asked.

"Yea, I have my gun in my waist," I said putting my hands on the back of my truck because I know that I'm going to jail.

Up until this point, I could say a lot of things about Lisha, but I could never call her a cop caller. The bitch never called the police on who she should have, Claud, but she called them on me.

"Sir, the gun is registered to her, and we really need to leave. My husband, her brother is in the hospital," Goddess insisted.

"These muthafuckas don't give a fuck about what's going on. They just want to take somebody to fucking jail!" Envii screamed, catching the people across the street's attention.

"Ma'am, if you could please calm down. We are just doing our job. We received a call about a disturbance and that Modesty was refusing to leave this residence. If you could just let us do our job then we can let you get to your loved one," the other officer insisted.

The officers made their way into the house, but all that I kept on thinking about was Gotti. Why the fuck is he in the hospital? Is he okay? Why didn't they call me and tell me what was going on with my brother?

"What's going on with Gotti?" I asked.

Goddess looked at Envii and then back at me but still hasn't said anything. *It can't be that bad or she wouldn't be standing here right now. She would be by his side,* I thought to myself while I waited for one of them to say anything. Envii has never been one to bite her tongue but for some reason, she hasn't said shit either.

"Gotti isn't doing good. He's been in the hospital since last night. I tried to call you, but you didn't answer. I texted you and got no response. Tasia and E are at the hospital, and I've been looking for you and your mom. Have you talked to her?" Goddess finally spit out.

"What the fuck is not doing good? What happened?" I asked as the officers came out the house.

"He had a heart attack," Envii said.

"A heart attack?" I questioned like I didn't hear what she said.

"Okay, Modesty. This is how it is going to go. They don't want to press charges, but I am going to have to request that you leave and do not return. Do not communicate with them in any way or we are going to have to take you in," the officer said as he walked over to us.

"Alright," I replied.

"What hospital is Gotti at?" I asked.

"University," Goddess said and I jumped in my truck and my phone started vibrating.

Looking at Messenger, I had a message request. I opened the message from Murk and it wass a picture of my son and a message saying *call me fucking now!* I instantly started seething and shaking because I don't know what the fuck this nigga might do. The fact that he is in Arizona and that close to my son scares me more than anything right now.

11

BIG FACE

"This is my cousin, Teflon," Sevino said as I nodded my head to Teflon.

I'm on my ass and now with Dani being in the hospital, I have to make shit shake. OG is doing alright but the stress alone could take her out. My momma been holding things together but barely because she had to be seen by the fucking doctors after she passed out from being dehydrated.

"Why did Kurupt stop fucking with you?" Teflon asked.

"Some shit with my cousin," I replied, confused because I didn't come here to talk about Kurupt.

"For what we are offering you, what can you offer us?" Teflon asked.

"What are you asking fo—" I attempted to say as Shnikia came busting into Sevino's office.

This bitch. As if this was the fucking time to come in here with her bullshit, but it's clear this nigga doesn't have any control over his bitch. And clearly they want to know information about Kurupt and his business. Shit went sour from Ace fucking Ahmina, but I know that double crossing niggas like them could fuck over my whole family, and that isn't some shit that I'm willing to do. My phone started vibrating and it was a text message from Kurupt telling me to meet him on Arapahoe and Gartrell Rd at the Maverick gas station. *How the fuck does this nigga know where I'm at?*

"When y'all ready to discuss business, call me, Sevino," I said as I got up to leave because I don't have time to wait for Sevino and Shnikia to finish arguing.

"I don't give a fuck what you're doing! Answer my fucking question!" Shnikia screamed as I made my way out the office and down this long ass hallway to the front door.

I came here to get the location for a pick up, but clearly this was just some shit trying to get information out of me, so Teflon can try to get back at Envii because she left him and went back to her husband. As I made my way to the car, my phone stated vibrating again. This time with a text message from Brionna and a picture of an sonogram. This bitch just won't catch a fucking clue. I haven't seen or talked to her in five days since she left the house. Shit, I thought that she had finally just let a nigga go. But, no, she still on her bullshit. Yea, I was fucking Brionna ,but I never fucked Brionna raw after I found out she was fucking that other nigga. There is no way in hell that she is pregnant with my baby, but she still keeps going on with this bullshit. I texted Brionna back.

Big Face: Congrats to you and Bad News. I'll send you a gift by my momma.

I made my way to the Maverick to meet Kurupt. I'm sick of talking to this nigga. At this point, whatever the fuck he plans on doing, we can just get to the shit because right now I got a lot of other shit to deal with. When I pulled up at the gas station, Kurupt was sitting at the picnic table that faces the street. I pulled next to where is GLK, white Mercedes was parked, jumped out and made my way over to him.

"So, are you doing business with them niggas now?" Kurupt asked before I could sit down.

"I have to eat. I have a family that I have to provide for," I replied.

"Them niggas just want to try to use you to see what you'll tell them. It's some personal shit that don't have nothing to do with you or me. You didn't have shit to do with what happened to my sister. Being a man, I made mistakes, even though it took some time for me to realize that, but I fucked up. I'm not gon' lie, I didn't want my sister nowhere near no nigga, not just Ace, but she made the decisions that she made. If you want to eat, you're welcome to come back to the table under one condition."

"And what's that?"

"Bring me their girls," Kurupt suggested.

"I don't even know who Teflon's girl is. So, you trying to use me to get them now?"

"Teflon doesn't have a girl, he's still heartbroken over Envii. I want his other girl. Not at all, this is business. I already made a call to get Dani and Ace moved out of Denver Health and and my wife to check on OG and make sure she has everything she needs. My shit is the best that you're going to get and you know that. And one more thing."

What I can't figure out is why this nigga wants to throw in the towel. Why does he want to let me back in. He knows that I come as a team with Ace. Is this a set up? Is that nigga just trying to set me up? Is fucking with him going to set me back up for life or is it going to fuck me over and everybody that I love?

"What, leave Brionna alone?"

"She was yo' bitch first, and to be real with you, what you do with that woman ain't none of my business. That's some personal shit and this is business. That nigga wouldn't miss her if she was gone. If you care anything about her, you might want to check on her."

"Why do you want their girls?"

"I need what is most important to them. I don't give a fuck

about his love for Envii. They are trying to fuck with my money and have been failing to pay the tax."

"Who is Teflon's other girl?"

"His momma. I have to go and pick up my daughter from school. If you can, show up tomorrow night at Gotti's spot," Kurupt said, standing up.

I jumped in the car trying to think about my next move. Ace has always been my right hand and the only nigga that I trust with my life. To be able to pull this off I need to have somebody that I can trust and isn't scared to put in work by my side to pull this off.

My phone started ringing and it was my momma. I answered the phone as I pulled off from the gas station and headed to OG's so I can see Ace and Dani because I haven't seen either one of them since they have been in the hospital.

"Are you sure this is a good idea?" My momma asked.

"Momma, I don't know, but shit, what other options do I have? I really don't know if I should fuck with them other niggas."

"Desperate niggas make desperate decisions, but before you come here, I need to tell you something."

"Momma, I don't need no more bad news."

"Who the fuck keeps calling you that you are fucking ignoring?"

"Modesty, I fucked her and now I guess today she decided to keep calling. She been calling all damn day."

"What day is her day?"

"She ain't got no day. Now what the fuck is going on?"

12

MODESTY

"Why is he plugged up to all these machines?" I asked as I sat next to Gotti's hospital bed.

"He's in a medically induced coma, ma'am. The doctor will be in soon to talk to you guys. Is there anything that I can do for you guys?" A nurse asked.

"Unless you can make my brother walk the fuck out of here, quit asking me that," I spat and got up to go and get some air.

My attitude isn't with that lady, she's just doing her job, but my mind is in so many places. If Gotti was out of here, I could focus on my other problem; Murk. I knew that Murk wasn't just going to walk away quietly, that isn't his style. But bringing my son into this, I didn't see coming. He knows what my son means to me. He lives with his dad Darius in Arizona. I'm not able to provide the stability that his father can, but I talk to my son every day, see him as much as I can and financially provide for him.

My son is three and Darius and I dated in high school. He is an ex hustla. When I found out that I was pregnant, Darius changed and was given a full ride scholarship to Arizona State to play football. His dad lives in Arizona, so it worked for him. I tried to take care of Lil Darius by myself, but it was too much. I was overwhelmed and I couldn't do it. I trust Darius and his family just as much as I do my own, so I didn't have to question if my son would be in good hands.

Murk knows about my son because when I was pregnant, Murk stopped talking to me. And he has gone with me to Arizona a few times but was never near my son. Murk and I used to be good friends. Other than my family and Mina, he's the only other person that knows about my son. I know that when people find out about me having a son, they will judge me and think that I'm a horrible mom. I did what was best for my son and Gotti didn't agree with it, but he didn't have a choice but to let me do it because no matter how hard he tried he couldn't control that.

"What's wrong?" Murk asked as I walked into the waiting room.

"Murk, please not right now," I replied as I kept walking, so I could go outside.

Me being here with Murk right now is just what I have to do. If he is here with me then he is nowhere near my son. I would much rather be with someone else, but I don't know how to get rid of Murk. I can't even go to my brother. Even though me and my brother don't agree on most of the shit that I do, I know that whenever I need him, he's there. He'll get up in the middle of the night to come and see about me, cut a vacation short to come and make sure that I'm good. Even if I'm on some bullshit and most of the time it is my fault, he doesn't give a fuck, he's going to come through.

"I'm here for you and whatever you need. I got you, Mo," Murk said as he grabbed me and kissed me on the forehead.

He's so damn bi-polar. One minute he wants to kill me and the next minute he can be the sweetest ass hole I've ever met. I looked up and the heat smacked me in the face as we walked out the hospital, and Envii was speeding into the parking lot. If

Envii could make Murk disappear than I would tell her that I want to be done with him, but she has no control over him. Even with her being his cousin and she being his boss there is nothing that she can do to control him. He doesn't listen to half the shit says.

"I have to go and make a run, you want anything?" Murk asked.

"Naw, I'm good."

"Call me if you need something."

I shook my head as I tried to think about what the fuck I'm going to do. Murk made his way to his truck and I plopped down on a bench in front of the hospital. I have to get away from Murk but I also have to think about my son and his well-being. My phone vibrated and I dug through my purse trying to find it.

Murk: Stay the fuck away from that nigga Big Face. Don't even think about that nigga! I'll kill you and him!

In a matter of minutes, he switched up. He just was willing to kiss my ass in any way possible and begging me to eat my pussy in the parking lot an hour earlier, but now he's threatening to kill me. I can't say that I'm surprised because he has been talking about Big Face so much, I couldn't get him off my mind if I wanted to. I haven't called him even though I wanted to until today and his muthafucking ass won't even answer my calls. Here I am being threatened to stay away from the nigga. Not to mention he wouldn't even come near me since I'm with my family. Before Big Face went to jail, we were tight as hell, but it's looking like fucking just brought us even further apart. I had feelings for Big Face before we fucked, but when he said that I would never be his girl, that shit kind of hurt. As much as I played that it didn't, I wasn't expecting him to say that.

"It's hot as fuck out here. Why the fuck are you out here?" Envii asked as she walked over to me.

"I'm sick of sitting in there," I admitted.

"You should be sick of Murk's sorry ass," Envii suggested.

"Man."

"Come on. I ain't sitting in this damn sun because you can't leave a dumb ass nigga that ain't gone ever change."

I got up and Envii lead the way up to Gotti's room. I'd been calling my momma, but I'm not even surprised she hasn't even bothered to call back. Even after all that Gotti's does for her. Gotti will get up and still bust his ass to make sure my momma is good. Meanwhile, she trying to get high knowing her.

"I need a nurse! Help!" Goddess yelled into the hallway.

I ran, pushing Envii out the way. I need to get to my brother. He's all that I have. I wouldn't be able to do life without him. We've had our issues, but my brother loves me and other than my son, he's the only man in my life that truly does. Once I made it to the room, I ran to Gotti's bedside and he's awake. I dropped to my knees thanking God for sparing my brother's life again.

"Modesty, Modesty, sweetie. You have to move so the doctors can check on him and unplug all the cords he didn't already unplug," Goddess pleaded, rubbing my damn back.

"Alright, G," I said, getting up.

That's her thing, she loves taking care of other people even when she needs help herself. She struggles with her addiction to heroin and unless you've been there when she stumbled you wouldn't be able to just look at her now and see all that she's been through.When Gotti killed her first love a few years back she spiraled out of control. Even though her and Gottis had been together for so long she was not at peace with her choosing him over her ex lover. That just so happened to be our uncle. don't know where she gets her strength from, but I pray that one day I am as strong as she is. Wiping the tears that fell, I sat down and Goddess started rubbing my back.

"G, I'm good. Where is Tasia and the twins? Damn," I said and she backed up from me.

"They are with Kai," Goddess replied, and she leaned against the wall doing something on her phone.

"Are you working right now?" I asked, knowing the answer.

"Get the money first and last," Goddess said, not looking up from her phone, quoting Gotti.

"Yea, get that fucking money because I ain't going nowhere but closer to retirement, my" Gotti said as I jumped up.

"Genesis!" I exclaimed, calling Gotti by his government that he hates since our father named him.

"What are you doing here, runaway? After a few hours in jail, you decided you want to come back home?" Gotti asked, removing the oxygen mask and then putting it back.

"Fuck you. I can't reach yo' momma," I said, sitting on the right side of Gotti because Goddess stuck by Gotti like his left hand.

"She in the hood trying to get high," Gotti said, rubbing Goddess's thigh.

We all laughed because we know that our momma is somewhere trying to get high but niggas know better than to serve her. Gotti will not only kill them, but their whole family. He gives my mom her high. Why, I don't know; only he could answer that. I never understood that and I know that I never will, but he's been there through all my bullshit, so I'll never question that.

"Hello," I said, answering my phone.

"Modesty, you need to get down here. Lil D is in the hospital," Darius said with worry in his voice.

"What is wrong with my baby?" I asked and cried into Gotti's shoulder.

Gotti snatched my phone like only he can do. He put the phone on speaker and Darius is calling my name.

"Modesty, you have to stay strong. I'm here, but I want you to be here. We found out that he has diabetes. He's stable now and he's going to be fine, but I want you to you to be here, so we can learn more about the treatment he is going to need," Darius said into the phone as I cried into my brother's shoulder.

When I was in college, I was trying to get into the nursing program, so I know about diabetes. Not to mention, Gotti and my mom are both diabetic. I never thought that my baby would end up being one too. All his physicals and six months check-ups, I'm there. I have to get my baby back home with me.

"She's going to be alright, cuz. Let me see nephew," Gotti said, Facetiming Darius as I laid my head on his shoulder.

13

BIG FACE

"I think your cousin, I know your cousin was back on that shit before she got shot," my momma said, opening a bottle of wine.

"Once she's good, I'll get her back in rehab," I replied, rubbing my hands over my face.

I got up from the kitchen table and made my way to Ace's room where he is set up at. OG is keeping him on life-support. I am starting to give up that my nigga is going to shake back from this. Dani, she's going to be good. Dope fiends shake back from every damn thing, so I know that she'll be good.

"Baby, we need you. That girl that you love, her and her daughter need you and your daughter," OG said as I walked into Ace's room.

The daughter she is referring to could be mine, she could be several other niggas. It's a lot of niggas that could be her father. We passed Jessica like a hot potato. We just passed her to Ace a few times, but that bitch is in love with me. She loved me so much that she kept fucking Ace trying to make me mad. All it did was make her want me even more. I'm not against wife'n a bitch, but I'll never wife a hoe.

"I'll let you talk to him alone," OG said, getting up and hugging me tight.

"They offered us our seat back. I don't think we should fuck with them other niggas. They too messy. They can't even keep they bitches in line. So, I can't take no chances. Nigga, it's sink or swim around this bitch. Dani back on that shit, so I'm gon' do what you would do when she come thru like she always do. I'm gon' get her right and send her ass off. I got Zay, well shit, me, momma and OG. Shit, I got to get this money until you come back. Nigga, you got to come back. We got to get our matching beamers and get a compound for our mommas and us to live on because I need my space from my momma, so she damn sure can't live with me."

Knock, knock, knock.

"Can I come in?" Uncle Lu asked, peeping his head in.

"You know my cousin don't fuck with you," I said because I know he don't want him in here.

"Look, Caleb. I fucked up and that is some shit that I'll always have to live with, but I'm trying to make shit right. I put this family in a position that I never wanted to. I fucked up, I got caught up," Lu said, coming into the room.

"Lu, not right now. If I don't know nothing else, I know my cousin, and he doesn't want you here right now unk," I said. Lu threw up his hands and made his way out.

"Shut the fuck up, nigga, I got you! I can't do this shit without you. This was yo' dream, you just brought a nigga along. I wanted to play football, you wanted to hustle. After I fucked up my knee, I just joined the family business. Nigga, I need you to wake up! Nigga, we need you!"

❧

SITTING in front of Gotti's spot weighing my options. I fell asleep next to Ace's hospital bed and l when I woke up and seen he was still fucked up, I decided to come here. I slept the whole damn day away and nobody bothered to wake me up.

"Fuck!" I screamed, hitting the steering wheel.

What if these muthafuckas is trying to get close, so they can kill me? If I don't get back down with them, it could make it come quicker. I have to hold shit down for my family. I'm all they got. It's only one other person that I can trust with my life, so I had to call her. Surprisingly, she answered.

Tap, tap.

I looked over and she was tapping on my window. I unlocked the door, so Brionna could get in. We just sat staring at the spot for about two minutes without saying anything. I don't know what is going through her mind, but I'm just thinking about my family.

"Why did Kurupt say I needed to check on you?" I said, examining her for new bruises or marks.

"He what?" She asked, scared and looking around.

"What the fuck are you looking for, Ike Loraine?"

"What exactly did he say?"

"You can come home," I said, staring her down.

"Are you going to change?" She asked, finally looking at me.

"Brionna Janae."

"Caleb Omar!"

"Did I ever not come home at night? Did you ever need anything when you were with me? Did you ever end up in the hospital because of me? Have I ever given you some shit? Look, I am who I have always been. I'm never going to just be with one woman, but that has changed the way that a nigga feels about you."

"So, that's a no, right?"

"Brionna, this is what it is. And if you can't live with that then you don't want me, stay with your abuser," I said and got out of the car.

I knew that she wasn't going to say that her and that nigga's baby are going to come home. After Bri left, I never fucked her raw on me! I just had to ask one more time. That will be the last time that I play myself over her or any other bitch, even the only one that I have ever loved.

~

"Nigga, I didn't know if you were coming?" Gotti mumbled under an oxygen mask.

"Nigga, what the fuck happened to you?" I asked, walking in and looking around.

"Not taking care of myself, but now I'm on this diet and exercise shit. I checked myself out of the hospital. I don't believe in that shit that K do. I ain't having nobody in my house regularly that ain't family or on my payroll," Gotti said as he flopped down on the couch.

"Nigga, you sure you don't need a doctor or some damn body?"

"Nigga, I got who I need right by my side," Gotti said, patting his tool on his hip.

"Alright, my nigga," I said, sitting down across from him.

"What the fuck is up with you and my sister?"

"Nothing that is going to come in between our business," I admitted.

"I'm not Kurupt. Modesty was my baby before I had one. If you're not trying to be the one to walk in my shoes when it comes to her, then you need to just stay the fuck from around her."

"Alright."

"I'm going to give you the information that I have and every-thing else is up to you. If you need anything then I suggest you steal it because this is your last and final chance to show that you deserve a spot at the table. Bring the bitches and you'll be paid per Kurupt because I think your life and yo' family's is payment enough."

14

BRIONNA JANAE MATHIS

"What the fuck is taking him so long? Did they kill him and are they coming to kill me and our unborn child next?" I said to myself out loud while looking around and gripping my tool.

Constantly checking my phone to see if Brandon is calling has become a habit that I can't shake. He thinks I'm in the hospital and didn't bother to even come and see me once. When I was sneaking around to be with him, he was everything that I ever wanted. Once he got me, he showed me that his hood name fits him well, and he's fucking Bad News. None of his family even fuckwith him, but his crazy ass sister and that is because that bitch is just as crazy if not crazier.

I love Caleb, but I got tired of begging him to change. Through all the shit that we've been through, he plays roles good as hell. I always knew that whenever he left the house and was "working", there was a good damn chance that after he finished, he'd be knee deep in somebody else's pussy. Whenever we went out to eat, he would have his phone face down. His phone would ring damn near non-stop and unless it was one of his people, he'd never answer in front of me. I done found so many hotel keys in the laundry, I could have started a fucking collection. Caleb provided for me in a way that no one ever did. When our son passed away, he put everything on hold to be there for me in any way he could. If I ever needed him, he'd drop everything to be there for me and my sisters. My only issue was with him now, and then were his bitches. My phone started ringing. I answered it before it could ring once good.

"Hello," I said.

"Where the hell you at? Have you talked to Big Face?" My sister Qui asked, and I can hear my momma in the background talking her shit.

"Tell momma to shut up. Yea, I'm with him right now," I said putting Qui on speakerphone.

"Are you taking yo' ass home?" My momma asked.

"Momma, no, I'm not going back there if he's not willing to change. Why would you want me to be with somebody that is going to constantly cheat on me? Not to mention he's denying our baby," I cried out.

"Well, I would be denying the baby to. You live with a whole other nigga and you just ruling him out like you know for sure that it's his. You need to let Maury figure out who the father is because that thumping in yo' cat is some other shit, not a DNA test!" My momma yelled.

"She might as well had called me if she had so much to say," I said, reaching into the glove compartment for a napkin.

"You know how momma is, but she is right, sis. Why are you even with—" Qui attempted to say before my momma cut her off.

"Yea, that's what the fuck I want to know. Why the fuck is you with Tragic Disaster?" My momma yelled.

"His name is Bad News," I said for the hundredth time since I've been with him.

"Horrible news, Tragic Disaster same fucking thing. Answer my damn question, Brionna?" My momma screamed.

"Just come home. I know that momma is irritating, but just

come home. You don't have to deal with his shit. Nothing is worth dealing with the shit that he puts you through. I understand why you don't want to be with Big Face, but Bad News is way worse, sis. Just come home. Have Big Face drop you off over here," Qui pleaded.

I looked up and Gotti and Big Face were coming out the front door of the spot.

～

"So, what's the plan?" I asked, breaking the awkward silence as Big Face and I sat down the street from Teflon's momma's house.

"Put these on," Big Face replied, not even looking at me while handing me a Walmart bag.

"What the fuck I need scrubs for?" I asked while putting them on.

"The bitch that came out of there earlier you thought I was trying to fuck that I told to meet me in thirty minutes, I took the bitch work ID's. Just don't put on her name tag. Go in there and make up some bullshit, you good at that. And when I ring the doorbell, let me in. I'll text you to make sure that everything is good," Big face replied, finally looking at me and handing me the shit he took from that bitch.

I snatched the cards and id from him and got out the car, so we could get this over with. I knew that he was going to act like this after I didn't just give in and say I would take him back. I never thought that I would leave him. Him, my momma and my sisters damn sure didn't see it coming. It's not an easy decision to live with and each day that I keep holding on to the pieces of him that I have, it gets harder, but I have to let him go. After I do this, I'm done and I am going to walk away for good.

Knock, knock, knock.

What the hell is taking this lady so long to come to the

door? Does she have a fucking walker? These tight ass scrubs. He could have gotten the next size up, clearly he can see that I'm not the same size I was. I should have just put on the pants because this tight ass top is uncomfortable as hell.

"Hello," I said as this woman that looks in wonderful health to me answered the door.

"And who the fuck are you?" Ms. Dawn questioned, looking me up and down and taking off her glasses.

"I'm Katie Johnson. I'm here because Faith's car broke down while she was running errands for you," I said because clearly this bitch doesn't give a fuck about this badge I'm wearing.

"So, they just sent some random here?" She questioned.

"No, ma'am, I'm on call for emergencies like this one. Anything that you need done, I am able to get it done for you," I said, hoping this bitch slow down with the questions and let me in. "Well, ma'am, if you don't need our services today, I'll just call my supervisor and let her know," I said and turned to leave.

"Kelly, come on and I'm checking yo' pockets before you leave because you ain't stealing none of my shit. I know that bitch Faith was fucking with my shit," Dawn said as I turned back around and she moved from in front of the door, so I could get in.

"Okay, what do you need me to do?" I asked, looking around to see if anybody else is up in here.

"Finish my damn kitchen that Faith half-ass did," Dawn spat as I texted Big Face.

I made my way down a hall, hoping the kitchen was in this direction because Dawn damn sure didn't offer to show me where it was.

"Don't take all damn night either, my grandbabies are coming soon!" Dawn yelled from the other room.

Big Face needs to hurry the fuck up. What the fuck is taking him so long? He probably is entertaining some bitches outside instead of in here getting this bitch, so we can get this shit over with. I turned on the water in the sink and texted Caleb again and he isn't responding. Now somebody is knocking at the door and all I can do is hope it's not her grandkids.

"Kelly, what the hell are you doing? Come get this damn door!" Dawn screamed.

"Here I come," I said, running to the door.

"Get on the fucking floor!" Big Face barked as I opened the door.

"What the hell is going on?" Dawn yelled. I screamed and rolled my eyes at Caleb as he brushed past me and went storming in the direction her voice was coming from.

I made my way outside and jumped in the driver seat of the car, then I heard a few gunshots ring out. And the neighbor's dog started barking. For this nigga to be the nigga Caleb claims he is why the fuck is his momma still in the hood? It's so dark out and the streetlights don't even work on this block. I made it to the street to my car with the light on my damn phone. I popped the trunk and what felt like forever was only a few minutes and Caleb came out with Dawn over his shoulder. She ain't moving. Did he kill the bitch? The way that he just threw her ass in the trunk, she damn sure gone have a bad ass headache.

As Caleb jumped in the car and I pulled off down the street, my phone started ringing. I could feel Caleb staring at me, but I have to answer it. I took a deep breath and went to swipe to answer it.

"You think that shit is cool?" Caleb spat.

"Hey, baby," I sang looking at Caleb but talking to Bad News.

"Where the fuck is you at?" Bad News barked in my ear. From the way Caleb was shaking his head, I know he heard him.

15

AHMINA

"Mina," Kurupt yelled as he plopped down on my bed, pulling the covers from over my head.

"What?"

"Get the hell up! Nigga, you have a daughter that you have to take care of. Did you forget? Not to mention that nurse keeps coming in here to get you in the shower. You have to wash yo' ass. Laying in this damn bed ain't gon' make Ace get up no quicker. Let that lady be able to do the job that I'm paying for her to fucking do. I'm done letting yo' ass just stay in this room," Kurupt spat and stood up.

"Did you kill him?" I asked.

"Now you want to talk about it? Because when I tried to talk to yo' ass, you were acting like a fucking mute. Get up and wash yo' ass. I need you to ride somewhere with me."

"I don't want to go nowhere."

"I ain't trying to hear that, Ahmina," Kurupt said on his way out the door.

"You're going to have to be the one to explain this to Tiana!"

"I'm not gon' have to explain shit to Tiana about me doing

what the fuck needed to be done to make sure that her and her momma came back home safely. I have busted my ass to make sure that we are good since I was sixteen. I know that you've been through a lot. I've been through most of that shit right with you. When I chose this lifestyle, I never imagined none of this shit playing out the way it did. I'll never apologize to nobody for doing what the fuck I've done for us!" Kurupt spat, slamming the door behind him.

My phone vibrated, but I didn't know where the fuck it was. When I feel asleep, Tiana was watching a video on YouTube. Reaching under my bed, somebody knocked on my bedroom door.

"Come in," I said, hoping it is Cindy the nurse, so she can see if my phone is under the bed.

"Ms. Wright, are you ready now?" Cindy asked.

"Yea, can you get my phone? It's under the bed, and I can't reach it," I asked and without hesitation, she got it for me.

720-312-9985: Tell your brother I ain't dead and I'm coming for both of you bitches and my daughter gon' be calling another bitch mom!

"Kurupt!" I screamed because we need to talk now.

"WHERE ARE WE GOING?" I asked as Kurupt and I rode in silence.

"Just sit back and relax, damn. You been trippin' all damn day," Kurupt said as he merged on the highway.

When I told Kurupt about the message that Tycoon sent me, he told me not to worry about it, he would handle it and then just walked away. I don't know what the fuck happened outside of that Walgreen's. When them niggas came running in there and snatched me and Tiana up, I thought it was some bullshit that Tycoon had gotten into and was just preparing to die. Until Bad News' mean ass started talking once we got in the truck I was in. I knew that everything was going to be okay when Kurupt's voice blared thruBad News' truck.

"We're going to Re-Re's tomorrow for dinner," Kurupt suggested because I damn sure ain't going.

"I'm not going. Just bring me a plate."

"Who the fuck do I look like? One of them niggas that work for me that jump and run when you make a request. You're coming, ol' girl is coming to do y'all hair and shit."

"I'm not and you can't make me go. What are we doing in the hood?"

"Why did you start fucking with Ace?" Kurupt asked as we stopped at a red light.

"No matter how mean I was to him, he wasn't having my shit. How hard he goes for his family reminded me of you," I admitted.

"I got you, Tiana and the baby a place."

"Over here? We can't live over here."

"Why not? You want to date the help, shit, ride around in old ass buckets, eating noodles and shit. You can't be bougie when you are dating a nigga that work for me. He should have been treating you how to play yo' role. Back to the hood you go," Kurupt replied, laughing and putting the truck in park.

"We'll just stay with you until I finish school."

"No, y'all not. Kai is right, I have to let you go and find yo' own way. You have to be the woman that I raised you to be. I did a damn good job, minus you falling for a bum. Then a nigga that was supposed to be protecting you."

"K, we can't live over here."

"Girl, get the hell out the truck. Damn, my bad, you can't walk. Tricks seen you run into traffic and get hit by a car."

"Is that why you let Big Face back in?"

Kurupt didn't respond. He got out and popped the trunk, getting my chair. I can't believe that he is trying to make us move to the hood. How the fuck am I going to be a single mom with two kids? Tiana is so spoiled thanks to Kurupt and his niggas. I'm going to have to talk to Kai because she can talk him into just letting us stay with them. With the staff that they have at the house, I'll be able to have some help.

"K, did you kill Ace?" I asked as he opened my door.

"No, Ahmina. Damn, when is the last time you had a green smoothie? You heavy as hell. You not even that far along, damn," K said, lifting me out the truck and into my chair.

"Fuck you!" I yelled as I drove my chair over to the sidewalk and looked up at OG's house.

"Why would you bring me here. These people don't even like me."

"Kai's people don't like me either. Fuck them and his people too. I know it's just his Annie because OG is a sweetheart. She can cook her ass off too. I hope she cooked because Kai taking summer classes and shit, so she ain't been cooking. If it wasn't for Raisin Kane's, I'd be having chicken withdraws."

"You know how to cook and tomorrow is Sunday."

"That's exactly why we are going to Re- Re's."

"Why won't you move Re-Re out the hood?"

"I tried. I bought a house years ago. She is never going to leave grandma's house."

"I can't go in there."

"I think it might wake him up," Kurupt said, lifting me up from my chair and walking up on the porch.

"How y'all doing? Y'all just in time for dinner," OG sang as she opened the door.

"Good, how are you doing, Mrs. Miller?" K asked, as I took my hair out of my messy bun.

"Call me OG, Mina baby, how are you feeling?" OG asked as

she sat down next to me on the couch where K damn near threw me.

"I'm okay, how are you?"

"K, your plate is on the stove. I'll be good once my baby is up," OG said, tapping my knee.

"K!" I yelled because his ass disappeared to the kitchen.

"What pissy? I should have brought Cindy. You gone put my damn back out," K said as he came into the living room with his plate.

"I want to go see Ace," I said and started crying into my lap.

"That's why I bought yo' cry baby ass here. I should have kept yo' ass in the hood a lil longer. You soft as hell," K said as he sat down on the love seat across from us.

"Shut up. He's here?" I asked as OG rubbed my back and held me.

"Damn, I should have brought yo' walker," K spat.

"Yea, baby, let me help you down the hallway to his room," OG said as Kurupt jumped up.

"Biggie, come on, so I can eat," Kurupt said, lifting me up as I continued crying into his shoulder.

"Fuck you! Kai should have brought me," I said, wiping my snot into K's shoulder.

"We're not leaving the house again without Cindy's crooked eye ass," K said as he sat me in the chair next to Ace.

Kurupt made his way out of the room and back to his plate. Nigga got a whole chef that he pays for nothing because when he cooks, he doesn't even eat. He'll go to Kane's if Kai doesn't cook. Looking over at Ace just made me even more depressed than I already am. When I showed up at his doorstep, I never imagined this happening. I wanted us to work things out, raise our child together, and him help me to raise Tiana.

"Baby, please wake up. I can't do this by myself. I need you; we need you. I can't do this without you. I'll accept your child the same way that you accept mine. Whatever we have to do, we'll do it. Just please wake up," I cried into Ace's hand.

"Grrrrrr...Unnnn..."

"OG!" I yelled. Baby, baby! Hold on," I said as OG, Kurupt and a doctor came running into the room.

"I told you," Kurupt said as he came to my side.

16

ACE

"OG, I'm good," I said as she continued to hug me, just making the pain worse.

"Oh, okay. I'll give you some time to talk to Ahmina," OG said as she hugged me and kissed me for the hundredth time.

Looking at Ahmina just seemed so unreal to a nigga. When the bullets hit me, I didn't think that I would ever see her again. OG left out the room, leaving us alone and I could tell by looking at her that she's been crying. I never wanted to put her through none of this shit. She got her shit going on and I got mine but maybe this ain't our time.

"I should have kept it real with you and told you what it was with me and Jessica. It didn't mean shit to me, but I see know that shit fucked you up. When Jess had her daughter, she told me that she got a DNA test and it was Tycoon's. I left it alone because I wasn't trying to have a baby with her. I kept fucking her to keep her mouth closed. She knows some shit that could get me and my cousin sent away forever," I finally said, breaking the silence.

"You could have just told me instead of having me looking

stupid in front of yo' family. So, you never seen a DNA test and she could be yours, right?"

"She's not mine, she's Tycoon's. My family wants her to be mine. My momma wanted grandkids and for years we weren't able to see Zay. My momma loves everybody and she just wants me to settle down, so she fucked with Jessica. Jessica doesn't mean shit to me and never did."

"I should have let you explain what was going on. It's not your fault because of my current situation. I just want to work things out. Whatever we have to do, I just want to do it, so that we can raise our child together. Tiana loves you and I can't imagine you not being in our lives."

"Our what? I'm confused. You pregnant?"

"Yea, I wanted to tell you when I came to the house but with all that was going on and the cold shoulder you were giving me, I didn't get to tell you. I didn't want to tell you while we were both going through so much. It's my fault why things played out the way they did with you and my brother."

"Mina, I'm going to do whatever needs to be done to make sure that the baby, you and Tee Tee are taken care of. Right now, I have to get back right. I got a lot of shit going on and it's not fair to bring you into this shit with me. I just need some time to get my shit together. It's not you and that a nigga trying to leave you, but I can't be the man that you want or need right now. When I get everything back right, then we can try this again."

"How can you tell me what I want and need? So, what the fuck are you trying to say? You need to get yo' shit together and then when that happens, we can be together?"

"Look, I ain't trying to put you on hol—"

"So, how long is all this going to take? A few weeks, some months, a couple years! What the fuck am I supposed to be doing in the meantime? Sitting around waiting for you and then you might come around?" Mina screamed.

"Ahmina, calm down. If I'm not all the way right, how the fuck can I can be right for y'all? I know that this isn't going to be easy for you to understand. It's not gon' be easy for me, but this is what I have to do baby."

"Don't baby me! Kurupt!" Mina screamed loud enough for the whole block to hear her.

"So, you just gon' leave?"

"Yup, and let you get back right," Mina said as Kurupt came into the room.

"I'm ready to go," Mina said, doing something on her phone.

Kurupt looked back and forth between me and Ahmina confused. I knew that she wasn't going to be cool with this, but I have to get myself back right. I can't do shit for her or my seed if I'm on my dick and right now, that's my situation. Waking up and seeing her and Kurupt confused the fuck out of me. The last words that Kurupt and I shared weren't cool. I handled shit the wrong way and I know that, but I can't take that shit back now. I just have to move forward and get shit back on track. Kurupt didn't say anything, he just lifted Ahmina and took her out the room.

"What is going on, Aiden?" OG asked as her and Annie came into the room.

"I can't be with Ahmina right now," I admitted.

"Good, you don't need to be," Annie threw in.

"Shut up, you can't tell him who he can and can't be with. Get a man before you try to give some advice about a relationship," OG commented.

"When did you get a man?" Annie questioned which my attention.

"You got a man?" I asked.

I ain't ever seen my momma with nobody but Lu. I never even heard about her with nobody but Lu. When she is talking about back in the day, the only nigga she got stories about is him. So, I want to know who her man and the way Annie is looking at her, she does too. Or, she playing roles and she already knows who the fuck she's talking about.

"We'll talk about it later," OG said as somebody knocked on the door.

"Can I talk to Ace?" Kurupt asked as he came into the room.

"Yea, y'all go ahead and talk. We'll talk later," OG suggested and got up from my bed. Her and Annie made their way out the room.

When I woke up, the first thing I said to myself was this nigga helped me to live, so he could kill me himself. If we could have talked, I would have told him what it was. I should have had more respect for him and stepped to him before I ever even entertained Mina. Because of the way she reacted, I know that he got some shit to say about that too now.

"I fucked up, you hired me even with all the shit that went down between us when you could have killed me and my cousin. For that, I'll always owe you. All that you did for me and my family, I shouldn't have moved the way I did with Mina."

"I fucked up too and I shouldn't have come at you the way that I did. Mina's a good girl and any man would want her. All I ask is that you do what you're supposed to do and be there for Mina and yo' child once you get on yo' feet. I don't know what the fuck is going on between y'all and I'm staying out of it unless my sister or the kids are being involved in any bullshit. I didn't send nobody to hit you. I would have done it myself, that shit was personal not business."

"What's the deal now?" I asked because I need to know what the fuck is going on and how it's going down.

"You can get your seat back at the table. I just need Big Face to finish handling something for me."

"Then what?"

"It's time for some changes. You still want to play the game?"

"It's all that I know. I got a baby on the way that I have to take care of."

"Well get some rest, you're going to need it," Kurupt said, walking up to my bed and extending his hand.

"I need to find somebody."

"Who, Jessica?"

"She fucking Bad News, he got her out the way. When y'all finished, I'll give her to you," Kurupt said as I shook his hand.

"What is he supposed to be doing? Because I need that bitch now."

17

BIG FACE

"You done yet?" Gotti asked as his voice blared through my phone.

"Almost, I just need a little more time," I replied.

"Aight, when you finish, I need you to go to Arizona for me," Gotti said.

"I'll get with you soon," I said and we ended the call.

It's one messy bitch that knows everybody business and that's Red. I called her crazy stalking ass and she was so damn excited to hear my voice, she was willing to tell me whatever the fuck I needed to know. Her and Sevino's bitch our cousins, I found out and she told me she was staying at her moms, which is Red's aunt. I been sitting in front of this house for hours and everybody and they momma been in and out of this bitch. There is no way that I can go in there and get her ass and have that many damn witnesses. I need to figure out a way to get this bitch out this damn house and if I don't have to include Red, that would work best.

When my phone started ringing, I just knew it was Red's irritating ass, but it's my mom. I answered and I keep saying hello, but she ain't sayi nothing back. I keep telling her ass to just get a new phone, but she keeps talking that shit about that one works. Just as I was about to hang up, she finally said something.

"Where you at?" My momma asked.

"On my way home. I can't find this bitch," I spat, starting up the rental I had to get. After getting Dawn, I had to get rid of that car.

"No, you need to come to OG's."

"For what? I'm not hungry. I need to go home and get in the shower. I been looking for this bitch since last night."

"Ace is up, nigga, so bring yo' ass here!" My momma yelled.

I disconnected the call and made my way to OG's.

"Do you know why Gotti wants me to go to Arizona?" I asked Kurupt as me, him and Ace talked.

"Modesty is down there. He thinks that something is going on and she ain't telling him everything. With his health and shit being fucked up, he can't move like he wants to. We all are dealing with our own shit and all of us can't go," K said, leaning back in his chair.

"Alright, I got to go. Mina trippin'," K said as he got up.

"What's wrong with Mina?" Big Face asked me.

"I respect why you stepped back from Mina but, nigga, to be real, I don't know if you ever gon' get her back," K said and made his way out the room.

"I don't want to talk about it. Hand me that cane, we got to go and get this bitch," Ace said and scooted to the end of the bed.

"Nigga, don't you want to wait a minute and talk some shit out?" I asked.

"Nigga, I don't have a minute. They could be coming for me any time now."

"I need to tell you something, shit. Look, I don't know how you gone feel about this, but uhh—"

"Nigga, since when you become fucking shy? Spit it out."

"Lu got Jess."

"The least that muthafucka can do is hold her until we get this other bitch then," Ace said, standing up.

OG was begging Ace to stay home but from the look in his eyes, he doesn't want to hear that. I tried to tell the nigga but he not gon' listen to shit that I have to say. I thought he was going to go off about Lu, but he didn't. When I saw Mina crying in K's truck, I knew it was some shit, but I also know how my cousin is.

"Ma, talk to OG and get her to move from in front of the door," I whispered to my momma.

"Jessica called me. Do you want tell me if what she is saying is true?" My momma asked.

"Now is not the time to talk about what a hoe told you. Get OG away from the door," I said, pulling her hand to get her off the couch as she mugged the fuck out of me.

My momma snatched away from me once she was on her feet and made her way to get OG. Ace wasted no time walking out the door. He doesn't even know about Dani and I know he gon' trip when he hears about her. We've been through so much shit with her that I didn't think we would bounce back from.

"What do you know about this bitch?" Ace asked as I unlocked the doors to the rental.

"She's Red's cousin," I said as I started up the car.

"I don't care what you say, you love that hoe."

"No, the fuck I don't, but me and Bri done."

"Nigga, y'all been done. I don't know how the fuck you forgot that."

"Nigga, fuck you, that was still my bitch."

"I don't have time for yo' fucking delusions. We got to get

that bitch, so I can get this money for my seed!"

"Yo' what?" I questioned as I put the car in park.

"Mina's pregnant."

"She tells you that she pregnant and you break up with her. What type of shit is that? That ain't some shit that you would do. You good? I mean, I know that shit is fucked up, but we done made it through worse, so this ain't shit for us to bounce back from. You know how we get down."

"I don't want to talk about Mina. What this bitch look like?"

"Nigga, I just left from over here. Who knows how many muthafuckas in that house now? People been in and out that bitch all day, why the fuck you think that I ain't got her yet? Nigga, I know you think you Billy bad ass, but you ain't going nowhere fast even with that damn cane," I said, showing him a picture of Shnikia.

I caught Ace up with everything that has been going on. I tell this nigga all my damn business and all of sudden talking about Mina is off limits. I didn't press the issue because I know that he got a lot of shit on his mind, but I do too, shit.

"Somebody coming out the house," Ace spat.

"One, leg that's that bitch I got her," I said as I got out the car.

Shnikia was yelling into her phone and from what she's saying, she's definitely talking to that nigga Sevino.

"Bitch, I don't give a fuck what you say! Do what the fuck needs to be done or I'm don—" Shnikia was screaming until I hit her in the back of her head with my tool and her words were cut short.

"What the fuck?" Shnikia screamed out gripping the back of her head and her phone slid across the street.

"Shut the fuck up, don't say shit else," I spat pressing my tool to the back of her lace front.

"I don't know what bitch you thought I was, but you got me fucked up with another one for sure," Shnikia replied.

18

MINA

"Where is the place at?" I asked K as we sat in Re-Re's living room watching tv.

"We'll go and see it tomorrow when Kai gets out of school. Speaking of school. When are you going back?"

"I don't know, K, everything is different now. It was hard enough with Tiana. How am I going to do that with another baby? K, I can't walk. I know the doctor said that I'm going to walk again, but I can't even see that far away. I feel like I'm at a standstill and I'm never going to get anywhere."

"K, go and help Re-Re," Kai said as she walked in front of us.

"And what you gon' be doing? I think you need to go and help her. When is the last time you been in the kitchen?" K said, but he got his ass up.

Whatever Kai say, that nigga do it, whether he wants to or not. He'll do anything for Kai and if it's going to make her smile, that nigga will run and jump to get it done. I'll never have that and the sleep I lost last night over so-called love, if that's how it's going to be for me then I don't want it.

"Mina, I know that it hasn't been easy lately, but you can't give up. You know all the bullshit that I've been through behind a nigga. I didn't think that I was good enough to accept the love that Kamal was offering me, so I went back to a nigga that could have killed me. Most of my family still doesn't even talk to me but everyday, I get up and still find a reason to keep going. It's not easy and every day when I wake up to my family, I'm reminded of the family that I never had. Sitting over here with Re-Re is so hard. You have kids that need you and them alone should motivate you to do whatever needs to be done to make it. We are here for you and whatever you need, we will make sure that you get and you know that," Kai said, trying to soothe me.

"Kai, how did you get over D?"

"It took some time and for everybody, it's different. I'd be lying if I said that when I got back with K that I was over D, but I wasn't. I was dealing with him for so long and even with all the bullshit he took me through, I still loved him. K doesn't know this but I used to still answer his momma and sisters' calls. I used to go and see them, but most of that was because of my guilt for what happened to him."

"So, I'm gon' be stuck on him for years?"

"I think that things are going to work out for you. I don't know when he's going to come back, but he's going to come back just like K did. You have to give him some time."

That isn't what the fuck I wanted to hear. I need to talk to Mo. She's with her son, so we haven't been able to talk that much. Plus, she's with Murk's crazy ass, so if she texts me back, I'm lucky. I know that Kai and Kurupt made it through their shit, but that doesn't mean that Aiden is going to come back for me. I played back in my head everything that he said last night, but I still don't understand why we can't be together while we get our shit together. My phone started vibrating and it was Tycoon again.

720-312-9985: Have one of yo'servants bring you to meet me at 9 or my momma is going to kill you and your brother, just like she did y'all momma.

I showed Kai the text message and she started screaming Kurupt's name. Of course he came running like she was fucking dying. The way he runs to her gets on my damn nerves. I know that I'm just jealous, but damn, this bitch is okay, just trying to tell my damn business. I told K about the other messages and he told me that he would handle it. What is on my mind is the fact that he said she killed my mom. K said that our half-brother killed our mom but it's just the fact that Tycoon said that she did.

"Mina has to tell you something," Kai said.

"I'm going to go back to school," I said while looking at Kai.

If she wants to keep her perfect family at home, I suggest she keeps her mouth closed and takes me to meet Tycoon. And she can bring the gun she used to kill D with because I'm damn sure bringing mine.

"Good because you got to do something other than lay in the bed using my damn credit card," Kurupt said and made his way back into the kitchen.

"You have to take me to see him," I whispered to Kai.

"Mina," Kai whined as Hope came running in the living room whining.

Kai dropped everything to give all her attention to Hope. The love that Kai has for Hope is unreal. She treats Hope just like she treats her own kids. She's the mom that Hope never had and even though one day I know Hope will have questions about Quita, she can never say that she didn't have a mother because she had that and so much more with Kai. The look that Kai keeps giving me on and off, I know that she doesn't want to take me to see Tycoon but is going to make another sacrifice for the family.

Knock, knock, knock.

Damn, I was hoping it was just going to be us for dinner, but I know that's probably my brothers' friends and their families. Envii, Enforcer and they damn football team came piling into the house and Goddess, Gotti and their kids came in right after. Just before K went to close the door, he was stopped by some damn body else.

"Damn, I didn't get an invite to family dinner?" My aunt Shonda said with her son Shakim damn near stuck to her hip like always. Some parents want their kids to go off to college or get drafted to the NBA. Aunt Shonda wants her son to be hand-picked to be in the game. K doesn't even talk to Shonda because she always wants something and the number one thing is always getting Sha in the game. I haven't seen them in years and by the look on K's face, he damn sure doesn't want to see them now.

"Shonda, not now," K coldly said, standing in front of the door.

"This is my momma's house and you owe Shakim. If it wasn't for him, yo' workers wouldn't have been able to get Shnikia," Shonda spat and pushed past K.

K looked back at me and made his way outside with Sha.

"Damn, one of the princesses is down bad. All fucked up. That's what happens when you think you all that because you moved out the hood and had a baby by the real boss's son. And look at ya bougie ass now," Shonda said with her hands on her hips.

"Bitch, the only thing that is saving you from this princess beating yo' ass is me being in this chair. You're an old miserable hoe. Why are you so bitter and mad? We ain't never did nothing to you but still our name is always in yo' mouth!"

"Shonda, I don't know why your here because I damn sure didn't invite you. What you won't do is come into my house and disrespect my niece. If you can't just shut the hell up then you can get the hell out of my house!" Re-Re insisted.

"I'll shut up for now for you, Re Re," Shonda said as K and Sha came back into the house.

Re-Re stormed out of the living room and came back with my plate. My mom, Re- Re and Shonda were really tight when I was younger. When Re-Re went to the feds, everything fell apart. My mom got on drugs and things were never the same again. Shonda always hated us, but I never knew why and that wasn't some shit that I ever cared about. My momma always said that she was just mad and hating.

"Mina, you good?" K asked as he sat next to me and pulled my chair back to him.

"Yea, what did you and Sha talk about?"

"Some shit yo' baby daddy and em' did last night. They on their way here now. Let me tell you something. The girl that I wanted was the girl that didn't want me. The one that didn't want anything from me. The girl that wasn't naggin' me, blowing up my phone. Didn't want to be out in the club every weekend. Ace did the right thing by falling back. You spoiled as hell and that nigga ain't in no position to spoil you. He's cripple like you, give that boy some time."

"I'm not waiting for him," I said and went back to eating my food as Ace and Big Face came walking into the living room.

Ace hadn't even looked in my direction and everybody is just so damn happy to see him. K, pushed me as he got up to go and talk to them.

"Hey, Ace! Mina didn't tell me you were coming!" Re- Re yelled in excitement.

"She didn't know I was coming," Ace said as he finally looked over at me.

"Mina, I need to talk to you real quick," Big Face whispered as he walked up on me.

"He can come and talk to me if he has anything to say," I said and went back to eating my food.

"This ain't about that nigga, but clearly you need to talk. I ain't doctor Phil, so I can't help you with that. It's about Choco-late. What the fuck is going on with her and that nigga Murk?" Big Face asked, still whispering. But Envii heard him and her ass was all ears now from across the damn room now.

"Uh, come on," I spat as I made my way across the living room and outside.

"What, Big Face?" I asked and went back to eating.

"Is that her nigga? I don't give a fuck about fucking some-body bitch, but she told me she cut off all her niggas."

"You need to talk to her about that. I got my own problems and Chocolate can answer any questions about her. I'm not getting in the middle of y'all."

"Look, I ain't making her my bitch, but I need to know what I'm walking into going to Phoenix. She was cool, but I can't have no bitch that move the way she move."

"If that's the case then why are you asking me about Murk. You like her, but you still love Bri."

"This doesn't have anything to do with Bri. I just need to know what's really going on since yo' girl clearly a lying ass Sagittarius," Big Face lied.

"Yea, whatever you say. Mo really likes you and I know that you like her or you wouldn't have been spending all that time with her while I was down. Bri's not going to leave Bad News for you. You a hoe. She clearly is over yo' bullshit and wants somebody that can pay the cost and be the boss. Or maybe she just got tired of yo' games and yo' freaks. When you find some-body that plays the same game that you play, it's hard to deal with, but Mo... I mean, Chocolate is worth it."

"Until Chocolate get rid of that nigga, she can't even get one of my days," Big Face boasted.

"It sounds good, but you don't know what you had until it's gone. She down there in Arizona with Murk and you here waiting for Bri to call you," I said, laughing and made my way back in the house.

"All this family knows about is living lies. Ahmina is my daughter and Alice caught the right nut fucking my man Krack!" Shonda screamed as I rolled into the house.

19

MODESTY

"Come on, so we can go in this class and learn how to take care of our son," Darius said, tapping my thigh as my phone started vibrating.

Without even looking, I know that it's Murk, but I need to focus on my son and learning how to take care of him. I know that Darius is not going to understand, but I need to take my son home. I couldn't do it before, but now I need my baby with me to make sure that we are good. I'm thankful for everything that Darius and his family did, but I need my son and he needs me. We are at this four-hour class to learn about carbs and how to give Lil D his insulin. With him being in the hospital, the nurses have been handling all of that, but we are taking this class to learn everything that we need to know to keep my baby good and healthy.

Diabetes runs in our family. My brother has it and even his twins have it too, but I never thought that it would happen to my son. This hasn't been an easy pill to swallow, but I feel a lot better since I'm here with my son. D has been pressing hard, but we were never meant to be, we just happened. I was supposed to meet him and love him because without him, I wouldn't have my son. He thinks that we are going to live happily ever after and ride off in his Impala, but we aren't. He's being drafted into the NFL and I'm happy for him, but I want him to know that we can be nothing other than co-parents.

Darius has had a few girlfriends over the years, but none of them accepted the fact that we co-parent except Daisha, but because I'm in town, he's been spinning her like a spin top. I know that's because he thinks that we are going to be together, but it will never work. I know this is going to be hard for him to accept, but I know that I have to tell him. Time is dragging and I'm glad I have all of these brochures because I can't focus on anything that the instructor is saying. My phone started vibrating and I opened the messages.

Murk: The only reason while you're getting a pass is because of our son.

Murk: You better have yo' ass to my room and don't have on no panties when I get there.

Murk: Do you want anything from the store?

"You still fucking with Murk, I see," Darius spat, scooting his chair away from me and closer to the only white lady in the class.

"Quit acting like a broad," I suggested.

"I'm acting like a broad? I'm the realest nigga that you ever had and to be real, you gon' miss me when I'm gone," Darius insisted.

"Who is that, Daisha? Answer it because she loves you and you deserve to be loved," I requested.

"Daisha's dying, I have to take this," Darius admitted.

～

"GO ON BACK to that nigga Murk. I got my son like I always have," Darius spat.

"Are you serious?" I questioned.

"Yea, he'll be home tomorrow. Go to that nigga like you always do."

"Why are you always in competition with Murk? You're nothin' like him. Not to mention, who the fuck would want to be like him? I'll be to see our son tomorrow when he gets back to the house he lives in," I said, sending shots.

"His home, the only home that he has ever known," Darius spat.

"I know that I'm not going back home without my son but clearly, I like to fight," I said looking up at Murk as I walked out of my baby's hospital room.

"At least he knows what it is because you are always going to come running back to me," Murk said, taking me into his arms.

Since we've been down here, he's been cool, too cool. Something is up with him, but I don't know what it is. I haven't asked because I don't care to be honest. I just want to get through the next few days and to go home alone with my son.

"I got shit set up just how bitches like it at the room and shit for you. I have to make a run and then I'll be right back," Murk said as we got into the truck he rented.

"Okay," I replied as he jumped in and skirted off.

"What the fuck is wrong you? He good, right? That's why you down here to be with yo' son and you took that class and shit. So, what the fuck is the problem?"

"I'm just dealing with a lot right now. My son is sick and I got this case. I don't know where my momma is at. It's just a lot."

"I'll pay yo' rent for the next few months and don't worry about that case. You didn't kill no fucking body. You'll be good, I know that yo' brother can handle that."

"I don't need you to pay my rent, I got it," I lied.

"I'm trying. What the fuck! No matter what I try to do for yo' ungrateful ass, it's never good enough. All the shit that I do for you! You're complaining about shit being too much but you won't even accept what the fuck I'm offering. Do you know how many bitches would love to be with me right now? All the shit that I could be doing, but naw, I'm here with yo' stupid ass!" Murk yelled as he pulled up to the hotel.

I didn't say shit because what I want to say isn't going to do nothing but make this a longer than night than it is already going to be. My phone started ringing and it was Gotti, so I answered. I can't bring this to Gotti. He's dealing with a lot and I don't want to hear his mouth. I have to get rid of this nigga, so me and my son can live comfortable because as long as he's around, I'll never have peace. Why can't he just go and be with one of them bitches that want to be with him so damn bad?

"Chocolate!" A familiar voice screamed out as I walked into the Westin hotel.

This nigga just always has to be so damn loud. All the white people in the lobby were looking at him crazy. I'm surprised to see him, especially since the last time I saw him, he was on an ankle monitor and curfew, but now here he is. The last thing I need right now is for Murk to see him, so then we'll have to argue and fight about him. Not to mention, I haven't heard from him since we fucked and when I called him about some money on the floor, he never returned my calls or replied to my text messages.

"Do you have to be so damn loud? And what are you doing here?" I questioned once I got across the lobby where he was sitting.

"I came to see you," Big Face replied.

"Sounds, good. I got enough going on right now. I don't have time for yo' bullshit."

I walked away, leaving Big Face sitting where I found him and made my way up to the room. I texted Big Face, telling him to leave. He read my message but didn't respond. Murk doesn't intimidate well, until he started pressing me like this about us being together. When we were just fucking and keeping it moving, I could have a nigga for every day of the week and I damn near did, and he wasn't losing any sleep over it. My phone started vibrating and it was a text from Big Face.

Big Face: I'm not going nowhere, Chocolate. That nigga doesn't scare me. He's a bitch and the whole hood knows that!

ME: Why follow me to another state when I'll never be yo' girl?

Big Face: I had an opening, so if you act right and get rid of that nigga, you might can get some more of my time.

I knew it was going to be some shit, but right now, I don't need this. I was feeling Big Face but that shit that he said the last time we were together, I can't act like it didn't happen. What the fuck do I look like taking one of his days? I ain't never been that bitch and I'm not about to be that for nobody, even him. When I opened the door to the room, I couldn't believe my eyes. Murk ain't never did no shit like this before.

He has balloons and flowers all over the room and shopping bags. Murk done spent a few dollars on me and paid for some shit, but never nothing like this. I guess that's why he was in his feelings about the cold shoulder that I had already been giving him. This is nice and all, but this changes nothing between us. He's not the type of nigga that I can see myself being with, let alone being around my son.

I made my way to the bathroom and he had candles lit, rose peddles and a hot bubble bath. I love taking baths and Murk knows that. I slipped out of my clothes and into the water. I needed this because I need to relax and don't want to talk to Darius's sister, so I can't get no weed. I already smoked what I brought with me. I'm not smoking none of Murk's shit because then I'll have to hear a lecture about how I don't need to be smoking. My phone started ringing and it was Mina. I put her on speaker and I could tell by her voice that some more bullshit is going on.

"Cut, the shit. What's wrong, Mina?" I asked.

"Ace woke up," Mina said.

"Then why the fuck do you sound so sad? That's a good thing, right?"

Mina told me everything that went on with her and Ace and I'm surprised because that doesn't sound like some shit that Ace would do. I can tell from Mina's voice and everything she is saying that this is hurting her and she doesn't know what to do. I'm listening to her but to be real, I don't even know what to say because nothing that I say is going to make her feel any better.

"Fuck these niggas. We are going to boss up on they ass and get our shit together. You are going to go back to school and I'm going to figure out what the fuck I'm going to do."

"Why don't you just go back to school with me?"

"I never wanted to go to school, you know that. I was just doing it because Gotti said that I had to. I don't know what I want to do, but I know it's not that."

"What about opening a boutique? Bitch, if you can do what you did then you can make that shit happen and I'll help you."

"Naw, that's a lot of—" I attempted to say before somebody started banging on the room door.

"Who the fuck could be knocking on this door like this?"

"Maybe it's room service or something," Mina said as I threw on a robe and went to answer the door.

"It better be and or this muthafucka better be on fire the way that whoever it is banging on the damn door."

"Why the fuck are you banging on my door like this?" I questioned as I answered the door and looked into the eyes of a bitch I hadn't seen in a long time.

"Where the fuck is Maurice?" Lex asked.

"Not here, so I suggest you take yo' ass back to Denver and keep getting left on read like you've been doing."

"Funny that's what you want to think, but we both know what it is."

"What the fuck are you doing here, Lex?" Murk spat as he walked up on us, pushing himself between us.

This isn't my first run in with Lex. She's Murk's baby momma that just won't let go. A lot of that is because Murk keeps fucking on her, so she's holding on to getting her family back. A family that she only ever had in her fucking delusional head. He never fucked with her like that, but she always thought that she was something more than what she is. I never blamed her. I blame Murk because of him not putting her in her place.

"Bitch, get the fuck back home to my fucking daughter!" Murk screamed.

I finished talking to Mina because I don't give a fuck about Lex or Murk. She hasn't ever followed us out of town, but she damn sure doesn't mind pulling up. That bitch pulls up at restaurants, malls, parties and every damn where else.

"Who you on the phone with?" Murk questioned as he slammed the door behind him.

"Mina," I replied not even looking up at him.

"Tell her you'll call her in the morning," Murk demanded.

"Girl, just call me back since yo' damn daddy is home," Mina said and hung up on my ass.

I guess I was taking too long to take my phone off of my ear because Murk snatched it from in between my ear and shoulder and threw it. Luckily, it landed on the bed instead of in the wall. It wouldn't be the first phone that he broke. We can't ever just have a good night without some of his bullshit and he wonders why I don't want to be with him. I just don't understand why he won't just let me go. He doesn't want me like he claims he does. He just doesn't want anyone else to have me.

"What the fuck is the problem now? I know that you not trippin' because of Lex. You know what that is. She isn't going anywhere, she's my baby momma!" Murk insisted.

"Murk, thank you for all this. And thank you for forcing me to fuck with you even though I told you that I wanted to be done. Is that what you want to hear?" I said as I stood up from the couch that I was sitting on.

"Oh, you want to be done?" Murk asked as his phone started ringing.

When he pulled it out and I saw Envii, I knew he was about to answer it before he did. But when I tried to walk around him, he grabbed me putting me in a damn headlock. Envii is screaming, but I don't know what the fuck she's saying. I wish they would speed up this damn conversation. This muthafucka even had the nerve to kiss me on my head as I tried to squirm out of his grasp.

"Fuck!" Murk screamed as his phone beeped, signaling that Envii had hung up on him.

"Because of you and Lex, now I have to go back home because she done started some shit," Murk said, pushing me so hard that I crashed into the nightstand, hitting my mouth and busting my lip.

My blood started gushing onto the white robe that I have on. I can't do this shit no more and whatever is going to happen is going to have to happen because this will be the last time that this nigga ever puts his hands on me. I reached under the bed to grab my tool then came back up and pressed it against the back of Murk's head as he sat on the bed doing something on his phone.

"You need to leave. We are done. You can go out of here in one of two ways, in a bag or just walk out, and I never want to see you again," I said shaking.

Even though I'm the one holding the gun, I know who I'm dealing with. I'm not scared of much but this nigga gives me chills and not in a good way. Murk laughed but hasn't moved, and I know when he laughs in serious situations that he's pissed. He clearly thinks that I'm playing and isn't taking this as serious as he needs to. He got up slowly and I cocked my heat because if I need to shoot this nigga I will and deal with the consequences later.

"You gon' shoot me?" Murk asked as he put his hands in his pockets like he didn't have a care in the world.

"I'm not fucking playing. Just leave," I pleaded.

I let off a shot, shooting right past him, hitting the lamp that was sitting on the desk. Murk rushed me and he tried to take my gun from me. He's bigger than me and damn sure stronger than me, but it's more than just me that I'm fighting for at this point. Where the fuck is security? I know somebody heard the fucking shot. I kneed him in his balls trying to get him to let go of the gun and it went off again, this time thru the ceiling. This nigga not only didn't buckle a little but rushed me into the wall. The gun flew out of my hands and slid across the hotel room's floor. Even with how I'm fighting back, it's no match for Murk because the body shots that he is giving me, I don't know how much more I can take. Looking around the room, I looked for something that I can hit this nigga with to get him off of me. Murk hit me so hard in my face, I couldn't see straight. My knees buckled and I slid down the wall. Murk grabbed me by my feet and started dragging me. I want to scream and fight back, but I couldn't because the room is spinning.

"You stupid, bitch. This is the thanks that I get after all that I've done for you! You ain't nothing but an expensive hoe! I never should have fucked with you, like I did! I should have fucked you and passed you just like everybody else does you!" Murk yelled as he tossed me into the hallway, and the room door slammed behind him.

"Ma'am, ma'am? Are you okay? Somebody get some help!" Someone yelled.

I looked up and Murk threw all of my stuff into the hallway and hit me in my face hard with something. I rubbed my face with the inside of my robe trying to see who the fuck was around me, so I can get the fuck out of here. I looked up and Big Face was standing over me.

"I got her, she good. Mind y'all fucking business and get back to whatever the fuck y'all were doing!" Big Face demanded, but this white lady that was tending to me like a nurse didn't budge.

"Bitch, did you hear me, move the fuck out the way. I got her!"

"Sweetie, you don't have to go with this thug," the white woman propositioned.

"Bitch, you wish you could go with me," Big Face spat as he scooped me up off the floor.

"I need my stuff!" I yelled out as he carried me down the hall.

"Girl, shut up. I'm gon' go and get yo' shit. What room were you in with that clown?"

20

BIG FACE

"Do you ever shut up? Damn," I said as I the door closed behind me before she could answer.

I made my way to the elevator, so I can go and holla at this nigga. We ain't never had no issues before. We fucked some of the same hoes, but other than that, I never had any real conversations with the nigga. I know that he works for Envii and em'. He used to fuck with Bri's sister, but that didn't last long. I went to step off the elevator and Murk was stepping on.

"What's up?" Murk said as he slipped his phone into his pocket.

"Nigga, what's up?" I said, feeling the animosity in the elevator.

I pressed stop on the elevator. Before Murk could say anything else, I hit him and dropped his ass. I backed up, so he could get back up on his feet and he swung. I ducked and dropped his ass again, stomping him out as he curled up. This ain't some personal shit, this is business. I was asked to check on Chocolate because he was worried about her. I don't think that he knew she was with Murk and I only knew she was with him because his baby momma was whining about it to one of her homegirls when I seen her the other day.

"Stay the fuck away from Chocolate!" I spat as I kicked Murk one last time.

I know that this isn't over, I know that I'll see Murk around. We travel in the same circles, but I also know that I won't hear anything from any of them because I'm sure they don't know that they fuck around. I'm sure that if Gotti had anything to do with it, Murk wouldn't be anywhere near Chocolate. Let alone be kicking her ass and throwing her out of a hotel room damn near naked.

I pushed the button to get back to the floor that their room was on so I could get Chocolate's shit and I won't have to hear her fucking mouth about that. Even though I'm sure she'll have some more bullshit to say before the night is over. Damn, she only supposed to be here for two more days and this girl brought her whole damn life with her and a tool. Looking at this gun case, how the fuck was this nigga kicking her ass. With all the shit that she talks, I wouldn't think that she would be letting a nigga kick her ass, but I was fucking wrong. I gathered up all her shit and made my way back to the room.

"I'm cool, we'll be back in a few days," Modesty said as I walked into my room.

"You still fucking with that nigga Murk?" Gotti asked.

"Naw, why you ask that?" Modesty asked, staring at me like I told the nigga that.

"Because I want to know. Are you bringing Lil D back with you?" Gotti asked as I sat down on the couch.

"Yea, that's the plan, but me and D—" Modesty was saying before she slammed the bathroom door behind her.

I called to check on my momma and make sure everybody is good. Dani woke up. I'm sure Ace cussing her ass out was probably what woke her the fuck up. Her and Ace been going back and forth since she's been up. She doesn't think she needs help and she can handle it on her own, and he is ready to kick her ass.

"Momma, what's going on?" I asked as she answered the phone with an attitude.

"Sitting in the hospital with Brionna. When the hell are you coming back?" My momma questioned.

"What part of I don't want to hear nothing about her don't you understand? If you want to be her fri—"

"I don't know who the fuck you thought you were talking to, but I'm yo' fucking momma! You're not my daddy, Caleb, and you can't tell me what the fuck to do. And until you do the right thing and step up and be there for Brionna, I don't have shit to say to you. I don't give a fuck if it all falls down tomorrow!"

Beep, beep.

"Ain't this a bitch," I spat.

"One of yo hoes acting up?" Modesty asked as she came back into the room.

"Don't sit on my bed," I spat, texting Red back because I told her that I would see her when I got back because she gave me her cousin's location.

"Where the fuck am I supposed to sit then?"

"You can plop yo' ass on this couch, the floor, go and get yo own damn room. The choice is yours."

"What the fuck is this hole in the floor?"

"I'm guessing yo' nigga missed trying to shoot you. How the fuck did you end up fucking with that clown?"

"He used to be my friend, but when he wanted more and I didn't, it went left."

"Why didn't you tell me about yo' son?"

"My son isn't any of your concern. You're not my nigga and you made it clear to me that you'll never be my nigga, so it's none of yo' business."

"I knew about him and that is exactly what I was talking about, how you could never be my bitch. What type of mother would leave their child to go and run around the town thottin' around?"

"Fuck you! You don't know shit about me! Don't fucking question the choices that I made for my son! I did what the fuck was best for him!" Modesty screamed, snatching up her carry-on and running into the bathroom.

It ain't my fault that she a fucking bad mom. I knew about her son because I've heard Gotti and Kurupt talking about him before. Gotti talked bad about her. Shit, to be honest, I ain't ever heard him saying nothing good about her. He done gave her spoiled ass everything and all she does is fuck it up to run back to the hood. I'll never get that shit. Who the fuck wants to go back to the hood after they make it out? Nobody but her dumb ass.

I grabbed the remote and turned on the TV. I'm ready to get the fuck out of here and go home. The only reason why they let me leave the state it because I made up some bullshit about my great aunt not having too much longer to live and she talked to one of Kurupt's people out here who kept going with the lie. I had to piss, so I made my way to the bathroom. When I opened the door, I could hear Modesty crying. I took a piss and washed my hands and her cries are getting louder. I walked right back out the bathroom. I done held her ass when I should have let her ass cry and done been there for her, when I shouldn't have been. I'm just gone do what the fuck I was paid to do.

My phone started ringing and it was OG. OG knows that I'm out of town, so it must be some bullshit if she's calling.

"What's up OG?" I asked as I answered her call.

"You got some mail here that you need to see," OG whispered.

"I know you didn't open my mail. So my momma not talking to me, but she is opening my mail. What is it?"

"It's from the State, it's a petition for child support."

21

MODESTY

"Darius, we need to talk," I said as my baby ran out of the kitchen.

"About what?"

"I know that I wasn't ready to take care of Lil D when I first had him, but I'm ready now and he needs to be with me."

"You think that you can come to town for a few appointments, birthdays and holidays and just show up one day after four days and take my son?" Darius questioned.

"That's not the case and you know it. I'm there for my son and I'm not trying to take our son. I know that you are still a big part of his life. I know how much that means to him and you, but I thought that you out of everybody would understand why I need to do this."

"You think that I want my son to grow up around yo' brother and his thug ass friends? You think I want my son around niggas that helped to kill my mom? I barely want him around you. I let y'all come around and talk to him as much as you want tom but he's staying with me."

"My brother and his thug ass friends? That's what yo' issue is with D coming to live with me?"

"Well, that and the fact that you don't even have a job. You dropped out of school, what the fuck do you have? If Gotti goes to the feds tomorrow, you'll looe everything and where the fuck is that going to leave my son? You got all these different niggas running in and out of you. You think I want my son to be around that shit?"

"I'm taking my son. The son that on paper I take care of. You can see and talk to him whenever you want to, but he's coming home with me."

"I'll see you in court," Darius said.

"All this because I don't want to be with you?" I asked as I picked up my purse off the counter.

"Fuck you, bit—"

"Say it, I want you to and them thugs will make sure that you are never able to play football again. That's what it is. You rubbing me, hugging me, taking pictures of all us together. The pictures you got hanging up on the wall of us from over the years. The way you text me good morning every morning."

I walked out the kitchen, leaving D alone with his thoughts and made my way upstairs to get my son. I packed up all of his stuff and he already knew that he was coming with me.

"You ready?" I asked Lil D as I walked into his room and grabbed up the stuff that he wanted to take.

"Yea, I'm ready. Can we go and see Daisha before we leave?" Lil' D asked.

"Yea, we can, come on. Let's go," I said and we made our way down the stairs.

"You're not taking my fucking son. You can go, but he's staying here," D said as he stood at the bottom of the stairs.

"We've already had this conversation. Move so we can go," I insisted.

"Don't take another muthafucking step!" D growled.

"Come on, baby," I said and kept walking down the stairs as D pulled out a gun and pointed it at us.

"You're going to shoot me in front of my son?" I asked as Lil D clung onto my leg and cried out for his dad to stop.

"If I can't have you, nobody will," D said, cocking his tool.

Boom! Big Face kicked open the door and knocked Darius to the ground The gun fell out of his hand. I picked up my baby, walked over D and made my way out the front door, leaving Darius and Big Face alone. Big Face and I haven't said anything to each other since he questioned my motherhood. I don't have shit to say to him. He's doing his job and I knows he's being paid well to do it.

I got D in the backseat and got in with him. I texted Mina back and googled the address to the hospital, so we can go and see Daisha before we leave. She has been a big part of my son's life and I wouldn't take that from him because of how shit played out with me and Darius. As my baby cried asking me questions that I don't have the answer to, I didn't know what to say.

"Why did my dad do that? What is that man doing in there? Is he going to be okay?" Lil D asked.

"Everything is going to be okay," I said, not knowing if that's the truth or not as Big Face came out the house.

I put my phone in the holder and turned on the GPS, so I didn't have to talk to Big Face, just like I did before we came here. My phone started ringing and I didn't know who it was, but I answered.

"Hello," I said.

"Hi, I am trying to contact Ms. Williams," the woman said.

"May I ask who this is?"

"This is Audrey and I am calling from the Aurora police department. Is this Ms. Williams?"

"Yes, this is her."

"I'm sorry to tell you this, but I'm calling to inform you that you've had a fire at your home," Audrey said.

All I could think about is all that I have was in that apartment. Where are me and my baby supposed to live? All of the stuff that I just got for my son, everything is gone. The money that I have to my name besides the money in my purse. Clothes that I needed to finish selling.

"Ms. Williams, I know that this is a lot to process and I'm truly sorry that you and your family have to go through this," Audrey said, taking me away from my thoughts because I had stopped listening to all the shit that she was saying.

"Thank you for calling," I said, and hung up as Big Face stopped at a red light.

22

ACE

"Look, I don't want to talk to you about shit. Where is the bitch?" I asked.

"I know that I fucked up, and I made a lot of mistakes. I'm trying to make this right. It's clear that you are more alike me than you want to admit or we wouldn't be here right now," Lu insisted.

"Unk, y'all can talk out this shit at another time. Where is this bitch, so we can get this shit over with?" Big Face asked.

I should have done this shit days ago, but Big Face wanted to be here for whatever reason. Maybe he wanted to tell the bitch bye because I don't know why the fuck else he would be here. Lu disappeared into the back and came back with Jessica. She looked like she wass in good health. It doesn't look like she's missed any meals because she's a lot thicker than she was the last time I seen her ass. The way she was looking at Lu is the same way that OG was looking at him when he came to the house a while ago. She's definitely fucking him. I'm not surprised, that's the type of shit that both of them do.

"I know that I deserve this, but you can't do this," Jessica begged.

"It's a lil late for any that. You should have thought about that before you went to the feds," I spat.

"I won't talk. I'll do whatever you want me to do. We have a daughter that I have to be here for. Please don't do this," Jessica said, looking at Big Face.

"Bitch, I don't have no baby with you," Big Face spat.

"Yes, you do. Tamera is yours," Jessica pleaded.

Looking over at Big Face, he looked back at me. There is a chance that she isn't lying, but I don't care, she risked our freedom. Now Big Face is looking at more time than he'll ever be able to do and they picked me up yesterday, and I was indicted as well. So, I'm not taking no chances on her not coming through again because she gets in her feelings.

"I know that y'all don't believe me and I understand why. I loved you, Caleb, and no matter what I did, you wouldn't be with me. I did everything that I could to get you to choose me and you never did. That is the only reason why I started blackmailing Ace. I wanted to make you jealous and then I thought that you would come back, but you didn't. You chose Brionna over me like you always did," Jess whined, and I shot her in her head.

"You don't need the bitch to get a DNA test, but we need the bitch dead to make sure that we both stay free," I said and walked out the door.

Lu can handle the body. It won't be the first body that he had to get rid of. I have some shit that I need to handle, so Big Face needs to hurry the fuck up and grieve over his maybe baby momma in the car. As I walked down the stairs, Big Face called my name, but I didn't stop walking. I don't give a fuck about what him and Jessica had. He has more bitches than anybody that I know. He doesn't give a fuck about Jessica and never did. The way she was professing her love for him, she knew what it was.

"Nigga, I know you fucking heard me calling yo name," Big Face spat as he came out the house.

"We don't need to discuss shit around that nigga," I said as he unlocked the doors.

"If we don't finish handling this, Lu wants a fee."

"I'm not paying that nigga for shit."

Big Face didn't say anything. He just started up his car and pulled off. We were going to meet with Kurupt and right now, and that is the only thing that I care about. I finally got Dani to go to rehab and right now, I don't have to worry about her. Zay is good, Annie and my momma are looking after him. Dani isn't going to be too happy when she comes home, but I'll deal with that when I have to. I can't get Mina off my mind and every time I start to call her, I don't know what to say. It's nothing that I can say until I get my shit together. After all that we have been through, I can't even look at her. The only reason why I agreed to go to Kurupt's house was because she's not there anymore.

"What the fuck am I going to do if she is mine?" Big Face asked.

"Nigga, take care of her," I said as I answered my phone. "Is that who the child support petition was for?" I asked.

"Naw, some bitch that is out of her fucking mind."

"What's going on with Bri?" I asked.

"I don't fucking know. I don't have shit to say to that bitch. She's the reason my momma not talking to me, because of her bullshit."

"Why would she keep going with a lie saying that her baby is yours? That's not her and you know that she doesn't even move like that."

As we pulled up in front of Kurupt's, I watched Bri come out the house. And by the way Big Face skirted up close enough to hit her and slammed on the breaks just in time, he saw her ass too.

"You fucking asshole! It's bad enough you're denying your daughter and now you want to try to kill us too!" Bri screamed.

I got out the car and went into the house. I don't have time for Big Face and his baby mommas today. I rang the doorbell and Kurupt opened the door with Tee Tee in his arms.

"Ace!" Tee Tee said, greeting me.

"You remember this nigga?" Kurupt asked, laughing and throwing Tee Tee in the air.

Tee Tee looks just like Ahmina. I can't believe she remembers a nigga. It's been a minute since I seen her. I never wanted to be that nigga that was in and out of her life or her momma's because I know how that shit feels. I never wanted to hurt Ahmina and I know that I have. Even though I didn't do anything directly to Tee Tee ,me putting Ahmina through shit ultimately can impact her too.

"Nigga, I don't do domestic shit in front of my home! Quiet that shit down or deal with that shit in the streets and not where my family lays their head!" Kurupt yelled out the door and shut the door behind him.

"How's Mina doing?" I asked.

"She's good. I just got Tee Tee while she's at school and then she got a doctor's appointment," Kurupt said as Tee Tee reached out for me.

"Now you want the nigga to hold you too? You switching up on me for this nigga, acting like ya momma," Kurupt said, handing Tiana to me.

Big Face came in the house and flicked Bri off before he shut the door behind him. I know how that conversation went. When they were together, they were so cool. Bri was down from the beginning, but Big Face doesn't know how to be with one woman. He ain't never been with just one and that ain't something that I ever see him doing. Not even for the only one that he's ever loved.

"What do y'all think about Shakim?" Kurupt asked as we walked outside on his patio.

"He's cool. He damn sure came thru that night with ole girl," I said and Big Face agreed.

"Ain't he y'all cousin?" Big Face asked.

"Yea, something like that. I'll let Mina tell you about it," Kurupt admitted.

"What?" I questioned, confused as hell.

"It's a long story. I'll let Mina tell you about it," Kurupt suggested.

"She'll probably never talk to that nigga again. How did that shit play out with Sevino and Teflon?" Big Face asked, getting to business.

"It all worked out. That's part of the reason that I wanted to talk to y'all. What we discussed will be delivered once y'all give me a location. I need to know what's going on with y'all cases." Kurupt asked as I played with Tee Tee.

"Kurupt! Kurupt!" Kai screamed.

"Mr. Wright! Mr. Wright!" Silvia their nanny screamed as her and Kai came running outside.

"Kamal, it's the police are here. They are in the front of the house and we don't have much time if you don't come out the said that they are coming in," Kai said.

"Kai, calm down. Everything is going to be okay. Call Iman and my niggas," Kurupt said, kissing Kai on the forehead.

"Get with Gotti and E, and they'll get y'all right. I'll get at y'all," Kurupt said, nodding his head and making his way back in the house with Kai and Silvia following close behind.

"What the fuck is going on?" Big Face asked like I knew something that he didn't.

"Nigga, I know just as much as you do."

"You know that I'm not even talking to Mina, I don't know no inside shit. I do know that we have to get the fuck out of here without being in cuffs," I said, standing up with Tee Tee in my arms.

"Silvia, get all the kids. Kai, baby, I need you to calm down. Everything is going to be okay. Whatever the fuck they got ain't enough. I'm coming home, alright?" Kurupt insisted.

I tried to tell Tee Tee bye and hand her to Silvia.

"Noooo, Nooo!" Tee Tee cried out.

"Nigga, you can't take her. I ain't catching no kidnapping charge fucking with you. I already been through that shit with Modesty. I had to beat her baby daddy ass, so we could get out of there. I don't fight bitches, so you on your own on this one," Big Face said as he made his way through the house.

"Tee Tee, I'll see you later. You have to go with Silvia," I said, trying to reason with Tee Tee, but I wasn't getting anywhere because she wasn't trying to hear that shit.

"Ain't y'all both out on bond?" Kai asked.

"Yea," I replied.

"Go in the closet," Kai demanded.

"Do what?" Big Face questioned.

"Go in the closet and move all the hangers to left side and push on the right side!" Kai yelled.

We didn't have time to go back and forth with her, so Kai lead the way to the closet. Big Face, Tee Tee and I made our way in the closet and Big Face opened the wall.

"What the fuck am I going to do with a daughter?" Big Face asked as we walked into a room that lead to a whole other part of the house that I have never been in.

"Bri's or Jessica's?" I asked, but I was serious as hell.

23

AHMINA

"Sha, what the hell took you, so long?" I asked as Shakim got into the truck.

"Some shit went down with Kurupt and he's locked up," Sha replied.

"What do you mean he's locked up?"

"The police came to the house and picked him up. Gotti called me and had me doing some shit that Kurupt needed done. That's really all I know. You know they don't really fuck with me like that."

"Where is my daughter?" I asked as I called Kai and didn't get an answer, so I tried to call Silvia and she didn't answer either.

"She probably at the house with Silvia."

"Probably, nigga, I need to know where my daughter is at."

"Hello," Sha said, answering his phone.

"Why is nobody answering the house phone?" I asked like Sha knew the answer.

"Hun, this is Kai."

Kai explained to me that everything was okay and she was downtown with Iman, Envii and Goddess. She put me at ease letting me know that Tiana was at the house. My heart was beating so fast, I feel like it's about to jump out of my chest. My brother has been locked up before, but it's been a long time since I had this feeling. Knowing the life that he lives, I know that this is something that can happen. He always comes home, but that doesn't make this any easier.

"Are you going to the doctor's?" Sha asked. I nodded my head and kept talking to Kai.

Last night was my first night in our new place with me and Tiana. It wasn't easy and I know that it's not going to get any easier, but this is my reality. I know that I have to stay strong for Tiana and my unborn child. Kai is calm as hell and I could hear Envii talking shit in the back. Kai told me that she would call me as soon as she found out something and I ended the call.

"Do you believe my mom?" Shakim asked like this was the fucking time to talk about that.

"I don't know, shit. And right now, I really don't care."

My attitude wasn't with Sha. Sha is just doing what he is supposed to be doing. I called Mo and she didn't answer. Ever since she got back from Arizona, I haven't talked to her much. I know that it's a lot on her having her son full-time now, but it's been two days and she hasn't answered the phone. She'll text back once and then stops. She told me that she was done with Murk for real this time, but he is the only thing that would explain her disappearing act.

"Have you seen Mo?" I asked.

"Naw, I haven't. My baby momma was talking to her, but I think that was just about the shit that's going on with her and Darius about her son," Sha said.

Sha is a different type of nigga. His baby momma cheated on him, had a baby with another nigga, and Sha still stayed. He's not only taking care of his daughter with Honesty, but her son too, and he treats them both the same. Honesty is Tycoon's cousin and she doesn't like me. I know that has a lot to do with why she is always blowing up Sha's phone whenever he's with me. I don't give a fuck about Honesty and never have; she got an issue with her damn self because I don't give a fuck about her.

We made it to my doctor's office and Sha helped me in, using my walker. The doctor told me that I needed to start using it. Kurupt wanted me to still see his doctors, but I wanted to see the doctor that delivered Tiana. Nothing against his people, but I know and trust the doctor and his team. I trust the physical therapist, and I'm still going to keep seeing her.

I didn't have to wait because I was right on time with Sha being late. Soon as I walked into the office, they called my name. I just needed to meet with the doctor since I decided I wanted him to deliver my child. All they did was tell me everything that I already heard from Kurupt's doctor yesterday. I pretended to listen, but my head was somewhere else for sure.

After about forty-five minutes, me and Sha were walking out of the doctor's office as a white Tesla pulled up to meet us.

"Who the fuck is this?" Sha asked, gripping his tool.

"I think I know who it is. Get me in the car, I don't have shit to say to her," I said as who I expected, Lady Heroin, got out of the passenger side of the Tesla.

Sha helped me as Lady H made her way over to me. I haven't talked to Tycoon since the last time he texted me when Kai took me to meet him. He never showed up and I haven't heard from him since. I told Kai that I would fall back and let K handle it, so I'm trying to let it go.

"Ahmina, I know that you're upset about what happened between you and Tyreese, but I don't have nothing to do with that. I've been trying to get in contact with him, but he isn't returning any of my phone calls," Lady H said as she stood outside the door, blocking me from closing it.

"Did you kill my mom?" I asked because if she did, then we don't have shit to talk about.

"Ahmina, what are you talking about. Why would you even ask me something like that?" Lady H questioned.

"Could you move? I need to go and get my daughter. As I'm sure you already know, my brother is downtown," I said, not even looking over at her, but she backed up and I slammed the truck door.

"Do you believe her?" Sha asked.

"Shit, I don't know. I don't even know if Alice is my momma or not, but if she's here then my dad is here, so I need to talk to him. He's married to the bitch, so he should be able to answer some of my questions. You better be on yo' shit because one fuck up and yo' ass is out," I said, trying to warn him as Honesty's name popped up on the dashboard.

My phone started ringing and it's Goddess. I answered as I prepared myself to hear what she had to say about my brother. We have been through shit before and I know that my brother is coming home. He always comes home.

"What's up G?" I asked

"Have you talked to Modesty? We haven't seen her since she got back from Arizona. She was supposed to bring the baby to see us, but she hasn't yet. I'm starting to get worried because she's not answering the phone or responding to my texts," Goddess whispered.

24

MODESTY

"Momma, please don't start this shit. You know that I don't have anywhere to go. You know I'm trying to figure shit out. It's too many people at Gotti's house already. I can't put this on him," I said, tired of arguing with my momma.

"You so worried about Gotti and what you can't put on him, but you think you about to come back to my damn house and put it on me. You've been here two months and what the fuck have you figured out?"

"Momma, you know what I'm trying to do. So, what is all this for you, want us to get out?" I asked because if that's the case, then I need to be getting the fuck on and not talking to her now.

"Give me five hundred and you can stay," my momma said with her hand out.

"We'll go," I said, not knowing where the fuck we were going.

My baby is at school, so I'll figure it out once I get the fuck out of her house. She knows what my situation is and she still doesn't care. It's not like she was the best mother. You would think that she would want to redeem herself being a grandma, but I was wrong for assuming that. She has been cool and really hasn't been getting on my nerves like she normally would. And she had been cooking and spending time with Lil D and everything.

I know that Gotti would let us come to his house. I can't keep running to Gotti when shit goes bad. Because the fire department ruled that it was an arson, I still haven't gotten paid for the fire. Like a dummy, I took all the money that I had in the bank out because I didn't want Gotti dictating and watching my every move. I had it in the safe in my condo. They claimed that everything was damaged and wouldn't even let me go back in, but I know somebody got my money.

I haven't heard from Darius's lawyer, but I know it's coming. Especially since Daisha passed away yesterday. He's not going to just let me keep Lil D in peace and he just sees him when he can. The only thing that I can ever say Big Face did for me was prolong me having to deal with that. I know that D is still thinking about the ass whopping he got because every time he calls, he asks Lil D is he here or has he seen him.

"So, where are you going?" My momma asked as I opened the front door with some of our stuff in my hands.

"Does it matter? You don't want us here," I said and took the stuff to my truck.

~

"WHY ARE WE HERE? Why we ain't not going to grannies?" Lil' D asked as we walked into the room.

"We're not going back to grannies, but we'll be getting our own house really soon, okay?" I said as I turned on his game to keep him entertained while I called back Goddess and Mina.

I have him signed up for after school and I'm paying for that. With my money being tight and us not having a place to stay, I might have to take him out of that. But, if I do then that gives me less time to be able to come up with money. I told myself that with me bringing my baby back with me, I wasn't going to go back to my hustle, but when I got that call as we left Darius's house, I knew that I had to do something.

"Why haven't you been answering my calls? What's going on Ahmina? Are you okay? Is the baby okay?" Goddess asked as she answered.

"We're fine. We are good. I'm just getting used to do this full time and getting his schedule down and everything. I know that we were supposed to come over on Sunday, but I promise we'll be there this week," I replied.

If Gotti and Goddess could have it their way, we would be at their house every other day. I can't take my son over there like that all to just come home to the hood at my momma's. He was comfortable living with D, but now I just feel like I'm all over the place and maybe I should have just let him stay with Darius until I was all the way together. I can't admit that to my family and I damn sure can't even think about saying anything to Darius like that, so I have to figure this out. As Goddess and I talked, I'm listening to her and I know that she means well, but her and Gotti have done enough for me. I can't keep living off of them. I have to figure this out on my own. Gotti,got my charges reduced and I ended up just having to pay a fine earlier this week.

"Are you sure that you guys don't need anything?" Goddess asked for the hundredth time.

"Yea, G. We are good. We'll see you guys in a few days for dinner," I said as Gotti got on the phone asking to talk to D.

I made my way back into the room to give D, the phone and him and Gotti talked as I called Mina on my iPad. I know that I am going to have to hear Mina's mouth because I haven't been around much. She's been doing her thing with school and taking care of Tee Tee. I'm happy for her because after all the bullshit, she's finally happy again.

"Bitch, I don't want to talk to you," Mina said as she answered my Facetime call.

"Shut up," I replied.

"Where are you at? Did the insurance check come yet?" She asked.

"No, and shit, I'm starting to think that it's not coming. They can't just not pay you. You didn't set the building on fire."

"Yea, I know, but I know who did."

As Mina and I talked I started to feel relieved and not as worried, but my reality remains the same. Mina just stopped talking about Ace every time that we talk. I'm surprised because I know that she still cares about him, but she told me that she has to let him go because after all this time, he still hasn't come back.

"Come over, it's the weekend and Lil D doesn't have school tomorrow," Mina whined.

"We'll come over tomorrow. Have you talked to Kurupt?"

"Yea, but he's still not home. They won't even give him a bond. I just been staying busy because if I didn't, I would lose my mind."

"Did you and Shakim take the DNA test?"

"Yea, we took it today. I'm scared, Mo."

"I know, but we're going to get through this together."

"Bitch, who's texting you?"

25

BIG FACE

"I don't know why yo' momma still not talking to you. She is just being petty. After all the shit that she done did, you would think that she would just let you figure this out on your own. You have enough going on to deal with."

"She done been mad for a few days before, but it's been a minute, and she still doesn't want to talk to me. She won't take the house that I just bought her or car and she put all the clothes and shit I bought her in the sitting room," I admitted.

"Just give her some time."

"I am."

"She's not talking to you but she done became the a darn good grandma to Tamera," OG boasted.

"I'm not nobody damn grandma. I done told you, don't even refer to me to nobody else as a grandma," My momma spat as she came in the kitchen with Tamera.

I never wanted a daughter, but that wasn't what God had in mind for a nigga. This shit ain't easy but even though my momma ain't talking to me, she done damn near took over Tamera all while still not talking to me. They get along and my momma done fixed the attitude she had when I first got her.

I checked my phone to see if Chocolate texted me back, but she hadn't. We bought tickets to go and see Keith Sweat, Dru Hill and Ginuwine before I got locked up and shit. I had forgot all about it until Red asked me to go with her. I haven't seen or talked to Chocolate since we got back to Gotti's. She got her and her son in her truck, sped off and I haven't seen her since. The last time that we talked wasn't that fucking friendly, but at least she did the right thing and brought her son home with her.

I paid for my ticket, so I'm going with or without her ass; the concert is Sunday. I'm gon' give her ass a few hours to respond because being a full-time mom isn't some shit that she's used to doing. My momma done already claimed Tamera for the weekend, so I'm going out. I ain't been out in months. All my time has been going to grindin' and Tamera.

"Did you and Modesty make up yet?" OG asked.

"We ain't beefing."

"I don't know why you fronting, you really liked that girl. You need to settle down before your old and alone because Tamera is eventually going to go off and spread her wings too."

"I got a long time before that happens," I said while she trying to make a nigga older than I am.

"He's dumb. Clearly I made two dumb ass kids," my momma said, looking at OG as she came back in the kitchen.

"I love you too momma!" Nia yelled as her and Ace came walking in.

My momma looked at me in more disgust than she has since she hasn't been talking to me and stormed out the kitchen. OG jumped up, hugging and kissing on Nia. At least somebody is happy that she's home because my momma sure ain't.

Ace and I are finally back tight and shit is moving slowly. With Nia being home, my hands are going to be full. Next month, Dani is supposed to be getting out and them two together gon' have a nigga drankin'. Ace has been playing it cool, but I know that he's thinking about that shit too. With him having a son, he's been sleeping in the trap. He goes home to change his clothes and goes right back.

"Come on, we have a video visit with Kurupt," Ace whispered to me.

I got up and followed him onto the porch. He picked up Dani and took her to get herself together. I went to see her at the hair shop and ended up running into some bitches that I damn sure wasn't trying to see. I had to cuss out Tameika, put Chasity in her place and cut off Tiffany all in the matter of minutes.

"How's everything going at the spot?" I asked once we were out on the porch.

"Everything is good," Ace said as his phone went off.

"What's going on?" Kurupt asked.

"Everything is good," Ace said.

"Nigga, it must be with you. You cut yo' fucking hair and got yo' self together, I see," Kurupt replied in between laughing.

"Yea, it's coming together," Ace said, handing me the phone.

"But, nigga, you in hair shops causing scenes. Why can't you just get one bitch and calm down?" Kurupt asked.

"Damn, how the fuck do you know that?" I asked.

"Nigga, I'm locked up and all these niggas do is talk. How's your daughter doing?"

"She's good. Just trying to get used to this. I missed all the baby days for sure and trying to make up as much as I can," I admitted.

"I understand. Hope's birthday is tomorrow and I ain't gon' be there, that's fucking with a nigga. Don't miss no more important milestones, young nigga. I need y'all to go and see Iman. He'll explain the next move. I'll be home soon. Just keep moving like y'all doing and let me talk to Ace real quick."

"Have you talked to Ahmina?" Kurupt asked.

"Naw, she won't return none of my calls, but she texted me a picture of her sonogram."

"Well you knew it wasn't going to be easy, but shit, that's life. She is going through some shit since we found out that Alice wasn't her mom. But she's been holding her shit down and is back in school and shit, so I'm happy. If y'all need anything, get with Genesis or Elijah and they'll handle it. I'll see y'all niggas soon and y'all better be at my baby's birthday party tomorrow," Kurupt said. I let him know that I'll be there and Kurupt ended the video.

"Come out with me tonight."

"Nigga, I ain't trying to go out," Ace said, leaning back in his chair, rubbing his hands over his face.

"I know shit with you and Mina ain't right, but unless you're going to fix it tonight, just come with me. You need to take a break and I told Dani I would take her out."

"Ya momma getting on my damn nerves. I need a drink, can we go?" Dani asked as she walked on the porch.

"Rule number one, don't be showing yo ass tonight. Rule number two, nothing more than a friendly nod to these niggas. Rule number three, if you get to acting too crazy, we're leaving. Rule number four, if you drink too much, we are fucking leaving. I don't give a damn if yo' favorite song is on," I said laying out the rules.

"Yo' daughter is in the house, nigga. And I don't plan on being with y'all for long enough to be acting crazy. The only nigga that I want to see will be meeting me there and then I'm leaving."

"Oh, yea... one more muthafucking rule. None of them raggedy hoes that you call yo' friends ain't sitting with us, but Tonya can if she got herself put together. Then she can come sit on my lap," I admitted.

26

ACE

"Hi, Ace. Thank you for coming," Kai said as we walked into the party and she took our gifts from us.

"No problem," I said, looking around for Ahmina.

"She's not out here. She's in the back helping Hope finish getting ready," Kai said as she smiled and went on to greeting everybody else.

"You can go and play," I suggested as the other kids ran around the room.

"Naw, I don't want to play. When can I go back to OG's?" Tamera asked, turning to Big Face.

"We ain't going to be here long," Big Face said, hugging her and she moped over to a table to get a cupcake.

"Ace!" Tee Tee yelled as she came running towards me.

I looked across the room and Ahmina rolled her eyes at me as soon as our eyes met. I didn't know that she was walking again. I can see that she is still in pain, but she's fighting through it. I know the feeling because I ain't all the way back right, but I'm getting there. I know that now isn't the time to talk to Mina, but I'm just going to make it through this party and then deal with it.

"Come play with us?" A lil girl asked Tamera. She looked back at us sitting at a table. Big Face nodded and she ran off.

"What do you think about what Iman said?" Big Face asked.

"Shit, I'm down if you are. I need to get it all right now," I admitted.

"Let's get it, but what about Dani?"

"She gon' do what she gon' do as far as her fucking with that nigga Sevino, but she'll never go against the grain."

"You ain't fucking see my text message?" Big Face asked Modesty and caught the white people next to us attention.

I finished playing around with Tee Tee then looked up and Mina was smacking her lips standing over me. I ignored her as Tee Tee finished telling me about her new room. Ahmina was irritated but clearly tired, so she sat down in the chair next to me as Big Face and Modesty caused a fucking scene. I told that nigga to just give her both the tickets and buy another one but he wasn't trying to hear that.

"How are you doing?" I asked.

"I'm good," Mina replied coldly.

"Look, I know that now isn't the time, but—"

"You right, it's not the time," Mina said, standing up and reaching out for Tee Tee.

≈

"Did you try to talk to Mina?" Kai asked.

"Yea, but she didn't want to talk," I said as Kai walked us out the party.

"She's going to see Keith Sweat on Sunday. I know you going, everybody in the party knows you going, Big Face. You should go," Kai suggested.

"I'll think about it. If you need anything, we got you," I assured her.

"We are good. My husband is coming home."

"You're going to chase Mina with me at the concert?" Big Face asked as we walked to our cars.

"I have to go and handle something. I might, I'll let you know."

I have some unfinished business that I need to handle. When I found out that Kurupt wasn't the one that put the hit out on me, I knew somebody else did. I ain't got no enemies that I knew of at the time. My whole family been on my ass about how I been trappin' non-stop. I been trying to find out who shot me. The first person to come to my mind was D but I needed to make sure, so I did.

"You ready?" I asked as I answered my phone.

"Yup, everything is set," the caller assured me, and I ended the call.

I jumped in my car and made my way to my destination as my phone started ringing again. It was Dani.

"Wassup, Danni?"

"How could you do this to me? You know my situation, so why now, Aiden!" Dani screamed in my ear.

"Look, I'm not about to let you keep coming in and out of Zay's life. He needs consistency and you ain't in a position to give him that, Dani. I'm willing to do whatever the fuck it takes to help, you but you got to help yourself."

"Fuck you! I wish they would have killed yo' ass!" Dani spat and hung up on me.

I knew that she wasn't going to take it easy and it wasn't an easy decision, but when Zay begged me to not leave him again and to not make him go back and live with his momma, I knew that I needed to do what needs to be done. S,o Iman helped me to get custody of Zay.

I pulled up to the spot, honked my horn and D came out.

"Who's in there?" I asked as he got in the car.

"Shakim," D replied.

We rode in silence to where we were going. He hasn't asked

no questions and since I stepped to him about business, he never did. He was just so happy to be on again, but all I was doing was using him to get what I needed which was his sisters house. I got that. He helped to get shit back jumping and shit is going better than good. So good that Big Face and I are in a position that's better than before we fell off.

"Who lives here?" D asked as I killed the engine.

I didn't say anything. I got out the car and lead the way. I haven't been back to this house since I got rid of Jessica. I haven't talked to Lu since before I called today. I know that Big Face paid him even though I said not to. I'm going to have to talk to Lu to deal with my issues before my son gets here because I can't pass that shit down. I knocked once and the door swung open.

"Look, I know I fucked up. And I wouldn't have never gave the go to that shit, but my hands were tied. Tycoon stepped to me and threaten to kill my momma if I didn't try to get back right with you. I knew that y'all wasn't fucking with me and I know why, but I couldn't let him kill my momma. Nigga, you can understand that," D pleaded as soon as Lu closed the door behind him.

"Have you told that nigga any of my business?" I asked.

"Naw, I haven't seen him since that morning that you got shot," D replied and Lu sent him home.

"So, Tycoon is working with the Feds," Lu said, reading my mind.

"I didn't even know that he was out," I said, heading towards the door.

"Aiden, we need to talk," Lu said.

"Talk, I don't have shit to say," I said and sat on the arm of the couch I was next to.

"I fucked up and I made a lot of mistakes, some that ain't proud of. I was moving sloppy and I didn't think that I would ever get caught up. I was getting money and I didn't give a fuck.

My mistakes costed the only people that I cared about a lot. I know that I can't change the past, but I want to make things right now."

"I know you and my momma got something going on, and I can't do nothing about that. I want to see my momma happy and I haven't seen her this happy in years."

I got up and went into my pocket then pulled out an envelope with money in it for him getting rid of D. I tried to give it to Lu, but he wouldn't take it. I nodded my head and extended my hand. On my way out, I pulled out my phone to call Iman because I need him to find where Tycoon is at, so I can go and see him. He didn't answer, so I called Big Face and knowing him, I'm sure he in somebody else's bitch.

27

BRIONNA

"Are you going to tell me what is going on with you and Tragic News?" My momma asked as she came and sat down next to me.

"The same shit, different day," I said.

"You did some foul shit, maybe this is yo' Karma," My momma suggested.

"I did some foul sh...stuff because I left a cheater?" I asked confused.

"That's not what I'm talking about and you know that, but you left Big Face to be with a nigga that's way worse. I can't tell you what to do because you grown, and I know that you don't listen to shit I say anyways because of all the bullshit that you've witnessed me go through. I should have never exposed y'all to that. What I don't understand is how you go from wanting to be nothing like me to ending up being just like me. What is it going to take for you to leave that boy alone? What, you need to lose another baby? Because at the rate that you are going, it's nothing but God that you're still carrying that baby and you know it. Look at yo' face, Brionna," my momma pleaded with me.

"I can go somewhere else because right now, I don't need this," I said, getting up to leave.

"No, you can't, so sit the fuck down. The only reason you came here is because it is the only place you can go that he won't come after you. If you go back to him, you might not be able to leave again," my momma said and hugged me as I cried into her chest.

She's right and as bad as I didn't want to hear that, I needed to hear it. I don't know what to do. I don't have anything. I don't know what I'm going to do if I leave Bad News. How am I going to take care of my daughter? We can't stay with my mom. We can't get along; after so long we'll be fussing and fighting.

My phone started ringing, but without even looking at it, I knew it was Bad News wanting to apologize and try to beg me to come back home. Some type of home we have. All he does is run the streets fucking other bitches and put his hands on me. I haven't fucked him in months and because he's so fucking nasty and trifling, I ain't trying to fuck him.

"Maybe you should go to California," my momma suggested as she rocked me.

"I can't go there. I haven't talked to my dad in years and I don't like his wife."

"Well you have to do something because what you are doing isn't working, Brionna."

～

"Quita is locked up," I said to my momma as I ended my call with Quita.

"What are you telling me for? I can't do nothing for her. If she want to be a damn criminal than that's on her. These are the consequences," my momma said as she handed me a plate full of food.

"I ain't hungry."

"I don't care what you are. It ain't about you. The only reason why I keep letting you in my house is because of that baby. Unlike you, I'm going to make decisions based off of her."

I started eating as my phone started ringing and it was Joy. I answered and soon as my momma heard her voice, she left the room.

"How are you doing?" Joy asked.

"I'm okay, I just—"

"Tell her the fucking truth," my momma said, cutting me off.

I caught Joy up with my momma staring down my throat to make sure I was eating. She offered for us to go to the spa and even though I declined, my momma didn't for me. I told her that I would meet her there. I needed to make sure Quita got out because clearly my momma wasn't concerned.

"Hey, momma," Quita said as she walked in the house.

"Don't hey me, Orange is the new black. How did you get out?" My momma questioned.

"Murk came and got me."

"The least he can do since I'm sure he's the reason why you were in there," my momma spat and stormed out the room.

"Fuck!" I screamed as I stood up and a sharp pain went through my body.

"Bitch! Yo' water just broke!" Quita screamed.

"No, no, no. This can't happen right now. I'm not ready. I'm not ready," I cried out.

"Well, bitch, get ready because she's coming!" My momma screamed.

"Come on, we need to get her to the hospital," Quita suggested too loud.

"Don't raise yo' voice at me, dummy!" My momma spat.

"Please, y'all, not right now. Not right now," I begged them.

"Quita, will you go and get me and my baby's bags?" I asked

and Quita ran to get them as my momma helped me out the house.

My momma can't drive, so she got into the backseat of my truck with me and Quita came running out the house like a mad woman. My family is more excited about this baby than I am. I do want to have more kids, but the way that she was conceived, I'm starting to feel guilty about. I tried to call Big Face, but just like I figured, he didn't answer. I called Joy and my momma snatched the phone out of my hand as I got another contraction.

Quita drives crazy as hell, so in what should have taken thirty minutes, only took about fifteen and we were at the hospital with a few more tickets on my license plate thanks to my sister. Momma and Quita got me out of the truck and in the hospital. I looked over and I saw Bad News's truck.

"Did you fucking call him?" My momma asked Quita because clearly she seen it to.

"No, why would I call him?"

I don't care who called him, I just don't want to see him right now. When we walked in the emergency room, my momma and me both scanned the lobby, but I didn't see Bad News, so I started to feel a little relieved. I knew this wasn't going to be an easy situation, but I damn sure didn't imagine that when I looked over I would see Big Face sitting with a little girl that's clearly sick. I just closed my eyes, praying that my momma and Quita would lead me in the right direction.

28

BIG FACE

"Caleb, how many girlfriends do you have?" Tamera asked.

None," I replied as they called her name to be seen.

"That ain't what yo' mom said to OG," Tamera replied.

"Girl, just focus on seeing this doctor," I said as a nurse lead the way to a room.

My momma been blowing up my phone and Bri even called. I haven't heard from her since we got into at Kurupt's. My momma hasn't been wanting to talk to me, so I know she just calling to argue about something. OG called me saying that Tamera was throwing up and I went to get her and bring her up here.

"What, momma?" I asked as I answered the phone.

"Who the fuck do you think your talking to? What the fuck is going on with Tamera?"

"We are waiting to see the doctor."

"Give her the phone. I'm on my way up there, so you can go upstairs and see about your other daughter!" My momma yelled and I handed the phone to Tamera because I don't want to hear that shit she talking about.

"I think that she just has that bug that is going around," The nurse said as she took Tamera's temperature.

Today just ain't my fucking day. Tamera handed me my phone back. It started vibrating and it said Chocolate.

"Will you just give your ticket to Mina?" Chocolate asked.

"Damn, no hi, how are you doing or nothin'. I'm alright, my baby is in the hospital, but other than that I'm good."

"Can she get the ticket or not?"

"Naw, but she can come. I'll get her a ticket," I said, and she hung up on me.

"Hi, Mr.—"

"Just call me Caleb," I said as my momma came busting in the room like the police.

The doctor explained everything just like the nurse explained she just like the nurse thought she has a stomach virus. We waited in the lobby longer than it took for the doctor to come and see her. She not acting like she sick to me, she has my mommas' phone and is doing something on it. I just want to get the fuck out of here. The way my momma is looking at me she has other plans, but she gon' keep being mad because I'm not fucking with Bri.

⁓

"I can't believe I let you talk me into this shit," Ace said.

"Nigga, you'll be alright. She knows that I'm going, so she won't be surprised when she sees you."

"I don't even fuckin' like Keith Sweat."

"Well, nigga, I do and hope I see some new hoes up in this bitch," I admitted.

"Mina should have her ass in the house any damn ways," Ace spat.

"Did Iman find Tycoon?"

"Nope, and time is ticking. Yea, we got our charges dropped, but we need to get that nigga before he comes for me again."

"You're good and naked," I said to Chocolate as we walked up on her and Mina.

"How about you just don't say shit else to me for the rest of the night," Chocolate spat back.

"It's going to be a long fucking night," Ace and Ahmina said together.

We were late as hell, so when we walked in Ginuwine was already singing. I was able to get the seats next to me and Chocolate seat. They were high as hell and I don't know why because this bitch is damn near empty.

"Are you back with Murk?" I asked.

"Are you back fucking Bri?"

"Naw, we're done."

"Good for you, but I still don't give a fuck," Chocolate spat as she went back to singing along to Dru Hill.

"Nigga, that's why you wanted to come here, to argue with her?" Ace asked.

Looking back and forth between Ace and Ahmina, they were the only muthafuckas that don't want to be here. Ace brushed past me and went over to Ahmina. Chocolate walked past me rubbing her ass against me and disappeared in the crowd.

"I'll come back and get you," Ace said.

"Nigga, I'm good. Go and make up with ya girl," I said.

"He's not making up with shit. He's just taking me home!" Mina yelled.

I didn't even say shit back because I knew that Ace didn't want to be here. The faces Mina been making since we got here, she didn't want to be either. I just went back to listening to the music and Chocolate made her way back with two drinks.

"What the fuck are you doing here instead of being with my sister?" A bitch asked from behind me.

Before I even turned around, I knew that it was Kira, Bri's

sister.

"Why the fuck ain't you with her?" I asked as Mo turned around.

"You know she doesn't fuck with me like that, but you should be there. After all that my sister has done for you and this is how you do her. That's fucked up!" Kira screamed.

"Bitch, get out my face!" I spat and she backed the fuck up.

"What type of nigga wouldn't be there for their kid?" Mo asked, trying to be funny with some weird ass voice.

I ignored her ass and snatched one of the drinks out of her hand that she damn sure didn't have plans on giving to me. I need a fucking drink since nobody won't let me enjoy my damn night without talking about Brionna and her baby because it damn sure isn't mine. As I downed my drink, Keith Sweat finally came out.

I'd been drinking since I dropped Tamera off. Ace wouldn't even let me drive down here. My phone started vibrated. I'm sliding up in one of these hoes tonight. Chocolate kept looking at me, rolling her eyes, but I'd be lying if I didn't say that she wasn't looking good tonight because she is. She doesn't look like she had a son. She ain't got no marks like some brand-new tires.

After about thirty minutes, Keith Sweat was finishing up and we could hear him as we walked out of the Bellco Theater. Chocolate was still mad, but it can't be with me because I haven't done shit to her ass. She got all loud and wanted to argue at Hope's Birthday party and shit, but she should be over that shit by now.

"Where am I taking you, to the hospital?" She asked as we walked across the street to parking garage.

"Naw, let me see yo' phone because I don't want you saying shit to me on the way to my fucking location.

"Funny," Chocolate replied as she unlocked the doors to her truck.

29

MINA

"So, you're not going to talk to me?" Ace asked.

"What do you want me to say? You wanted to figure out where you wanted to be and get yo self together and now you want to come back?" I asked.

"Mina, I was in no position when you showed up to my house to take care of y'all. I couldn't be with you and be what you needed me to be. And even though you mad, you know that."

"What I needed from you was for you to be there. I needed for you to not just walk out because shit got hard. When you left your house, Tycoon had some niggas snatch up me and Tiana while you were doing who knows what!" I screamed.

"Mina, baby, I did not know that none of that happened," Ace admitted.

Tiana is with Kai and the kids and now, I'm wishing she was here with me. I should have let Ace take me to get her. The only reason why I agreed to let him take me home was because I didn't want to be at that damn concert. I only agreed to go because I know that Mo is going through a lot and she really wanted to go. I needed a break, but I would much rather be doing a bunch of shit other than that.

I said the bare minimum to Ace in the past hour we've been sitting in front of my house. He's been trying, but I'm not just going to wake up and be over what the fuck he did to me when he told me that he didn't want to be with me. Kai and Envii told me that he was back right and that everything would be working out soon, but I didn't think that he was coming to Hope's birthday party. I've been ignoring him and Lady H because I don't have nothing to say to either of them, but I have to talk to Ace rather I want to or not.

"I see that Tamera is Big Face's," I said as Ace stared off into space.

"Yea, we found out a few months back."

"Where is Jessica?"

"Dead."

I nodded my head and texted Mo to see where she is at because she was supposed to be coming here after the concert. I know it has to be over by now. She hasn't said anything negative about Ace since he came out of an a coma. I know he still doesn't like her ass because he didn't even speak to her and has no plans on speaking to her.

"Mina, I know that when I told you that I needed to get right, you didn't want that or understand why I needed to and I get that, but I'm going to do whatever it takes to make this work. I don't want shit to be like it was before because it was never right. I want shit to be better. I want to have a family and I want that with you and the kids. It might not be tonight or tomorrow, but however long it takes, I'm not going nowhere and I'm gon' be here. I love you, Ahmina."

I didn't say anything because I don't know what to say. What if I take him back and then tomorrow it all falls down? Is he going to need to leave to get himself together again? I can't go through that again. I need somebody that isn't just going to walk out when things get tight. I need somebody that is going to stay and fight and do whatever it takes to hold shit down. I got out of his truck as Mo pulled into my driveway like a bat out of hell. I know it's some bullshit with Big Face by the way she slammed her truck door.

"I need some time," I said then got out of his truck and went into the house.

"What the fuck is wrong with you?" I asked. I walked into the house and Mo was turning a bottle of Remy up.

"Why the fuck do I like him, Mina? I knew what the fuck it was. He doesn't give a fuck about me. Here I am in my feelings over a nigga and I don't know where me and my baby are going to sleep tomorrow when he comes back with me.," Mo said as I sat down next to her.

"It's going to be alright; I've offered you money and you won't take it. I offered you to stay here and you won't. Why don't you just call Gotti? Or call Goddess. She's not going to throw it in your face what you're going through, Mo. You just need a little help right now. Everybody needs help sometimes."

"Mo, I can't keep running to them. And when I went to pick up D from school, I got served. Darius is taking me to court to try and get full custody. How the fuck can I convince a judge that I can provide for my son compared to Darius? Not to mention I'm sure he's going to get to talking that shit again about my family."

"Did you tell Gotti about what happened with Darius?"

"No and Big ass couldn't have told him either, or he would have said something about it. I don't have no choice but to go crawling back to Gotti until I figure this shit out," Mo said and took the bottle to the head again.

"We talk our shit about them, but if it wasn't for our brothers, we would both be somewhere fucked off and fucked over. They have been there for us and even though they stay on our head, we can always depend on them to come through. And we can't start this boutique because I set up a meeting to meet with Goddess for Tuesday when I get out of school. So, we need to sit down tonight and think of some ideas, so I can send it to my friend from school that can draw us up a business plan."

Knock, knock, knock.

"Who is knocking on my door?" Probably fucking Ace.

"I told him that I needed time and here he comes back already," I said as I opened the door and was met by the barrel of a gun.

30

ACE

"Nigga, where the fuck is you at? I need to get back to Mina's." I asked Big Face's drunk ass.

"Sonoma Resort on Saddle Rock. Right by the entrance. Come and get me from this bitch house who lives in an apartment called resort and don't even got no furniture. Get me the fuck out of here. Chocolate would never," Big Face slurred.

"Nigga, why the fuck didn't you call Chocolate? She could have come and got yo' drunk ass."

"She told me she's never talking to me again and called me a dead-beat dad thanks to Bri's momma blowing up my phone and Kira's fake gay ass trying to check me at the concert."

"Nigga, maybe you need to get yo' self together and go check on Bri."

"Fuck Bri, nigga, that's not my baby for the last fucking time! Back to Kira. You know that bitch supposed to be gay now? You used to fuck that bitch. She ain't gay, she just homeless and that bitch taking care of her. Aye ,light skin, why don't you pretend to be gay and get you a bitch, so you can get some furniture?"

"Nigga, bring yo' ass outside, so I can get the fuck out of here."

"Alright, bitch, lose my number until you get some furniture!"

"Where you at, nigga? I don't see you?"

"You said by the entrance, nigga, walk yo' ass to the entrance. Maybe you'll sober up."

"Fuck you! Here I come. If you back in love after begging like my nigga Keith then why did you leave her house?"

"Modesty is over there and she told me that she needed some time, but we done had enough fucking time. We got to make this shit work," I said and hung up as I finally seen his drunk ass staggering through the parking lot.

I ain't seen this nigga like this since the night that Bri had their son. Even though he keep screaming fuck Bri, that can't be the case because he's clearly going through something. I know that him having Tamera has been something that he ain't used to, but shit, my momma and Annie been helping that nigga, so he ain't doing it on his own.

"You better not fucking throw up on me," I said as he got his drunk ass in the car.

"Nigga, this is my car. And, nigga, you ain't ever see me throw up drankin'. I know how to handle my liquor So, beggin' ass nigga, what's going on with you and Mina?"

"None of yo' fucking business."

"Just take me to Chocolate, I'm sick of you," Big Face said and turned up the music.

I'm taking his ass right to her. She can deal with them and get the fuck out of Mina's. I have to find that nigga Tycoon, but if he's working with the feds, it's going to be damn near impossible to get to him. Mina telling me what he did to her, that just made it even worse for him. When he found out about me and Mina, I knew that he was going to want me dead, but to do some shit to her and Tiana that was out of line.

We made it to Mina's and all the fucking lights in the house is on. What the fuck are they in there doing?

"Let me go get Chocolate, so she can take me to my next location," Big Face said, getting out the car. I jumped out right after him.

I knocked on the door and nobody came, I rang the doorbell and still nothing. I twisted the door handle and it opened right up.

"What the fuck?" I spat as we both pulled out our tools on this nigga Tycoon who had his pointed at Mina and Modesty.

"I knew you were coming. Her pussy's good, huh?" Tycoon asked. I shot him in the leg to sit him down and he tumbled over. I made my way over to Mina to check on her and make sure she was good.

"I'm good, I'm good. Just get him the fuck out of here," Mina assured me.

"Kill me! What the fuck you waiting for? Whether I'm here or not both of you niggas is dead!" Tycoon yelled out as Lady H walked into Mina's house.

"I knew you were going to eventually show up here," Lady H said as she sat down on the couch like we didn't have our guns pointed toward her son.

"Why are you sitting down?" Tycoon questioned, grabbing his leg.

"You working with the feds to testify against Kurupt. What the fuck type of position do you think that puts me in?" Lady H asked.

"I don't know what you talking about," Tycoon said, trying to stick to his lie.

"Nigga, don't try to play me. You got out early how again? You get pulled over by the police for reckless driving and don't even get a ticket. Then you have a shootout with Dro at Walgreens and neither one of y'all dumb ass niggas hit each other, just wasting bullets. You a fucking disgrace, no matter what the fuck I do to try to help yo' dumb ass. Now you a snitch? Like Father, like son," Lady H said. Standing up, she kissed Tycoon on the top of his head then pressed her tool to it and blew his brains all over Mina's wall.

"Mina, I'm sorry. My people will be here to clean this up. I got be honest,I did kill Alice. Alice was my friend and she betrayed me, so watch this bitch," Lady H said and walked out the house just as fast as she came in.

Mina got up from the couch and ran upstairs, so I went after her. Even though he did all the shit he did, he's still Tee Tee's father and she did once give a fuck about him. Then the fact that she admitted to killing Alice on top of that with no remorse. I don't even know what the fuck to say about that. I heard about her and I've seen her before, but I'd never seen her in action until tonight. Any bitch that will kill her son ain't got it all for sure.

"Mina?" I called out as I looked in the rooms for her.

"Ace, please just wait downstairs for them to come and get him and leave," Mina requested.

"Mina, I'm not leaving."

"Just please just give me some space! I want to be alone right now!" Mina yelled. I gave in and turned to go back downstairs, but I don't give a fuck what she said. I ain't going no fucking where.

31

MODESTY

I've been sitting out here for like thirty minutes trying to talk myself to go in here and talk to Gotti and Goddess, but I can't. I can't go back in his house and have to abide by his rules like I'm still a fucking child. I have a few hours before I have to go and pick up Lil D from school. I made a few runs today and even filled out applications for a job. I've never punched a clock and I never needed to, but now I'm running out of options and don't want to ask nobody for shit. I started up my truck and pulled away from Gotti's, making my way back to the hotel.

It was one thing running the streets and trying to get rid of merchandise by myself but doing that shit with my son just doesn't feel right. I can't have muthafuckas coming in and out of the hotel. I don't have nobody that I can trust in the hood to get rid of everything, so either way it goes, I'm fucked. I'm trying to get this money together, so I can finish paying this lawyer for the custody battle on top of that. My phone started vibrating. I checked and it wasn't my baby's school, so I didn't bother answering.

As I pulled up to the hotel and made my way in, it felt like I was in a daze. Just when I didn't think that shit could get no worse, it does. I put on a brave face because I didn't want my son to know the truth about what's going on, and I can't let my brother and em' know, but everything is falling around me. When I walked into my room, I knew that something was wrong. Nobody should have been in there because I put the do not disturb sign on the door.

As I went through the room, not only did they take a lot of my damn clothes that I had just got. They took my baby's game system and all the shit that I needed to sell to be able to pay for our room for the rest of the week.

~

"YOU HAVE to be here by six o' clock. If you're not here by then, I can't guarantee you and your son being able to get a bed," the woman said for the hundredth time.

"Okay, I got, it we'll be here," I said, looking up at the Family Tree house of Hope.

I talked to the manager at the hotel and they told me it wasn't anything that they could do about my stuff that was stolen. I could live with my stuff being gone but having to explain to my son about his stuff was what hurt the most.

"What are you doing over here, Chocolate?" Big Face asked as he pulled up to the curb on me and got this fucking house manager Susan looking at me crazy.

"None of yo' fucking business," I spat and jumped in my truck. The last thing I need is him in my business. He needs to worry about his own problems, instead of being in my damn business.

Looking back, Big Face was still in the same place, just watching me. As I pulled off, I saw him talking to a bitch that was coming out of the Family Tree House of Hope. He'll fuck anything. I don't know why I thought that we would ever be anything because clearly it was never going to be nothing more than just a nut to him then and now. My phone started ringing and it was Mina. I know that she would have just tried to talk me out of it, so I didn't even tell her that I was coming here.

I can't stay at her house with her, Ace and Tiana. I made my way to go and pick up Lil D from school because he'll be getting out soon. And if I'm not one of the first people in the line, he'll be asking more questions than he already will be once he finds out where we are sleeping tonight. This is temporary and if this doesn't make me get my shit together, nothing will.

When I pulled up to the school, I saw Big Face again, but this time talking to my son. I was even more irritated than I already am. Why the fuck is he talking to my son? Ugh, I don't have time for his bullshit today, I have enough going on. He needs to just go and see the bitch down the street where he had me drop him off to the other night.

"Yea, y'all can hang out or do something. We can go to Dave and Buster's now. Momma ain't got nothin to do," Big Face was telling Lil D as I walked up on them.

"You'll have to hang out with your friend some other time because we have some stuff to do," I told lil D and he sighed, making me feel worse than I already do.

"No, she doesn't. We are going right now. You can ride with us," Big Face insisted.

"I need to talk to you," I whispered to him.

"We can whisper to each other at Dave and Buster's, Chocolate," he replied and jumped in his car. Lil D looked at me for approval, so I nodded my head.

Soon as the kids were in the car, Big Face pulled off. I don't have no extras right now, but I couldn't not let Lil D go. Out of all the kids in this damn school, he had to become friends with Big Face and Jessica's daughter. All he's been talking about is missing his friends in Arizona and his teachers, so I'm glad that he found somebody that he gets along with. Soon as I got in the car and turned on my truck, the gas light came on and my phone started ringing.

"What's up, Gotti?" I said as I pulled off from the school.

"What's going on with you? I rode past yo' apartment to drop something off and I couldn't even get in the building. Where the fuck is y'all staying at? I know you don't have yo' son at momma's." Gotti questioned.

"Naw, we good. I'm waiting for the insurance check and we'll be moving into another place."

"When the fuck did this happen? Why wouldn't you tell me that shit happened? Y'all just need to come to the house while y'all waiting for all that shit to be handled."

"Gotti, we're good."

"Pick Lil D up from school and get to the house, Modesty!" Gotti yelled and hung up.

Ugh, I'm not going to his fucking house. I know that this is just going to start some shit between us that I don't need right now, but he'll get over it. I jumped on the highway to get to Dave and Buster's and my phone started ringing again. But this time it was my insurance agent. I hope she has some good news. Right now, that money would come in handy and get me into a place at least.

As the lady began talking, I knew it was some bullshit. She started explaining that my claim was approved, but it would be anywhere between four to six weeks before I would receive any funds. After she said that, I just tuned her out because anything else doesn't matter. Because the shit that she is talking about is not going to help me right now. I've already filled out all the papers that I needed to and paid my damn deductible which was five hundred dollars that I didn't have.

I pulled up to Dave and Buster's and Big Face and the kids were getting out of his car and running in. I had to have a pep talk with myself because I cannot break down right now. Not here. I can't let Big Face know that I'm going through any of this bullshit. I got out, grabbed my Dave and Buster cards out of the glove compartment and drug myself in. Lil D was smiling and so happy. I haven't seen that smile in a few days since his game was stolen. When my phone started ringing, I looked at it and it was Goddess. I know she's calling to try to be helpful, so I just silenced my phone.

"So, you gon' tell me what the fuck is going on with you?" Big Face asked as the kids started playing games.

"I'm good."

"Yea, that's why you look like you just rolled out of bed. Damn, I thought we were better than that. I know you a thief, but I never took you for lying ass bitch."

32

BIG FACE

"Why the fuck are you so concerned with me? I'm not one of yo' bitches," Chocolate spat and started doing something on her phone.

"You still want to be?" I asked.

"Fuck no, dead beat!"

"Hi Big Face," Red sang from behind me.

"Wassup," I said without even turning to face her.

She's been begging to meet my daughter, offering to do her hair and cook us dinner. This bitch is crazy and I should have never fucked with her. She thinks because she helped me find ol' girl that we are back to how we were, but we're not. No matter how mean I am to the bitch, she just won't catch a clue. This ain't no coincidence that she's here.

"Aren't you going to introduce me to your daughter?" Red asked, rubbing my back.

"Naw, get the fuck on," I spat, turning to face her, so she will know that I'm not playing.

"All you fuck with is begging ass bitches. Begging for you to buy them shit. Begging for yo' time. Begging to play step-mom."

"You want to be her step-mom? I'm having auditions."

"Nigga, quit talking to me," Chocolate spat and Red started fake clearing her throat like she wanted her audition.

"Let me holla at you over here," I said, stepping away so Tamera wouldn't hear me.

She already think a nigga got all these bitches thanks to my momma and Red just popping up all the damn time. I'm sure she thinks that she's more than what the fuck she is.

"Quit fucking just popping up on me. You not meeting my daughter, I don't want none of yo' fucking food. Nothing ain't changed."

"What about—"

"What about what? Bitch, I gave you all the time you are getting for what you did. Thanks, appreciate it. Now you can get the fuck on," I spat, turning my back on her.

"All this is because of her. That bitch ain't—"

"Bye, Red!"

I know that she ain't just gon' fall back, but I'll deal with her ass later. The kids kept playing and then Tamera started saying she was hungry, so I went over to a table and ordered our food while they kept playing. Chocolate wandered over to where I was sitting and sat on one of the stools with an attitude.

"You looking for a job?" I asked as I scooted closer to her and looked across the room. Red was just sitting at the bar staring at us like the stalker she is.

I flicked Red off and gave my attention back to Chocolate. Why the fuck would she be looking for a job? I've never seen her do nothing close to work, so I can't imagine her going to punch no clock.

"Ugh, if you must know, yea."

"Whatever happened to you starting up that boutique shit? I don't think you should do it with stolen shit, but—"

"Quit talking to me," Chocolate said without looking up from her phone.

"What's wrong with you? You need some dick? You on yo' period? What the fuck is wrong with you?"

They brought out our food and as I called over the kids, Chocolate started looking at me like I was crazy and embarrassing her. I don't give a fuck about embarrassing or these nosy ass people that's looking at me.

~

"YOU LIKE HER, DON'T YOU?" Tamera asked as we got into the car.

"Why you ask that?"

"Because of how y'all was acting. OG told me that you do and grandma said you ain't no good, you like errrbody," Tamera said, taking my phone out of the cup holder.

"I'm sick of yo' damn grandma."

"Can I play with Darius again soon?"

"I don't know, we'll have to see."

As I pulled up to my house, I saw my momma's car in my damn spot. She still claims she ain't talking to me, but she just shows up at my damn house whenever she feels like it. Tamera was happy to see her here. She jumped out the car and ran into the house, not even getting her backpack. I grabbed up her stuff and made my way in the house. As I walked in the house, I was surprised to see Bri's momma. My momma and her never really got along, so the fact that they are hanging out now is some bullshit.

"Tamera, go and get in the shower so you can get ready for bed," I said as I sat down to hear what they had to say.

"What's up?" I asked and rubbed my hands over my face.

"I know you and Brionna are done, and I'm not here begging you to get back with her, but your daughter needs you," Trina said.

"I'll go see Bri, and I'm taking the fucking DNA test. Y'all can quit talking this my daughter shit. There is no way that Bri's daughter is mine. She might want her to be mine. Wish upon a fucking start that she was mine, but she's not," I spat.

"Go take the fucking test then," my momma threw in as she kicked back in my fucking chair.

I got up and went upstairs to make sure that Tamera was good then walked out the house without saying anything to anybody, so I could get to the hospital. I'm so sick of this shit. I'll be happy when I don't have to hear about it no more. The quicker I get this DNA test done, the quicker I can get this shit over with.

It took me about ten minutes to get to the hospital and once I got there, I made my way in and they sent me up to labor and delivery where Bri was at. I wonder why the fuck her nigga ain't here. And that's the type of nigga that she wanted. When I got in Bri's room, she was sleep, so I just left her alone, changed the channel on the TV and pushed the button for a nurse.

"How can I help you?" The nurse asked as she came running in the room.

"I need to see about a DNA test," I said and she looked back and forth between me and Bri's back.

"Bitch, did you hear what I said? Just do yo' fucking job!"

The lady ran out the room and a few minutes later, another nurse came in and swabbed my mouth. This nurse didn't ask no questions but my name and birthdate, took my ID and had me sign the papers. My type of bitch; no back talk and no extra questions, just minding her business, doing her fucking job.

"What's yo' name?" I asked.

"Brooklyn," The nurse replied.

"You got a man?"

"Umm, no," She replied like she was nervous.

I wouldn't normally care if a bitch had one or not, but in my current situation with Bri, I'm leaving other nigga's bitches alone. Brooklyn and I exchanged numbers, and she left back out the room. I went back to watching tv and drinking coffee, trying not to fall asleep. It's been a long day and I know when she wakes up it's going to get longer. About an hour passed and Bri started tossing in her sleep.

"I'm surprised to see you," Bri said as she rolled over and laid eyes on me.

"I didn't want to wake you up," I said as I went back to looking up at the ceiling.

"I need to talk to you," Bri said, sitting up in the bed.

"We don't have shit to talk about. I took the DNA test, so I could shut up yo' family and mine, and I don't have shit else to say."

"It's no easy way to say this, but I stole your sperm and that's how I got pregnant with our daughter."

"You did what?" I asked, jumping up off the couch.

"I know that I shouldn't have done it, but you're the only person that I want kids with. You're the only person that I want to be with. I know that I made my decision and you clearly made yours."

"Why the fuck would you do some shit like that? How the fuck did you do that shit? Have a fucking baby with that nigga you're with!" I screamed, now standing over her.

"I'm sorry. I'm so sorry. I took one of yo' condoms after we finished. I tried to, but he can't have kids," Bri cried out.

"Save them fucking tears! Bitch, you should be in jail and if I was a cop caller, yo' ass would be!"

I stormed out the room. I can't sit in there with that bitch. Who the fuck does some shit like that? We talked about having another baby when we were together, but never when we were just fucking. She knows that's not some shit that I would have went for. Why the fuck would I want a baby with a bitch that I'm not even gon' be with?

I called my momma and she answered before the phone could even ring.

"Did you take the test?" She asked with an attitude while hitting a cigarette.

"You better not be smoking in my damn house. I bought you a house that you can smoke 'til you choke in. Yea, I took the fucking test and this bitch admitted to stealing my fucking condom!" I screamed the last part.

"She did what? No, the fuck she didn't. She wouldn't do no shit like that. That's not Bri, and you know that," my momma said, still standing up for this bitch.

"What the fuck is you looking at? Yo' momma should have swallowed yo' dusty ass. With them dry ass tracks!" I said to the bitch in scrubs that's been staring since I walked in this bitch.

"I'm going to take Tamera to OG, and I'm on my way up there," My momma said.

"No, you not. Leave my baby in her bed. It ain't shit that you can do to help."

My momma was still standing ten toes down for this lying, stealing ass bitch, making me madder than I already am, so I hung up on her ass. I called Ace because I know that he's not going to believe this shit.

"Nigga, do you know what time it is?" Ace asked as he answered.

"Yea, but I got a fucking emergency. I need you to come up to the hospital."

"Nigga, is you dying?"

"Naw."

"Is one of our people?"

"Naw."

"Then, I'm not getting out of the fucking bed."

"Nigga, I'm for real. I need you to come up here."

I told Ace the bullshit that I just found out, and he told me that he was on his way. I want to choke that bitches' neck. I should just take my ass home, but I'm staying here until I get the results. They told me that under the circumstances and the fee that I paid, I can get the results in twenty-four hours, so I ain't going nowhere until then.

∽

"NIGGA, this is crazy. She stole yo' shit and did what?" Ace asked.

"Nigga, had them freeze it and put it in her bitch ass. Nigga, what the fuck do you think?!" I spat as I kept looking at the DNA test results.

"You okay?" My momma asked as she sat down across from us.

"What you think?" I asked as I got up.

"You need to go and talk to her," my momma suggested.

"I need to go get my daughter and go home, that's what the fuck I'm 'bout to do."

"Don't you want to see yo' daughter?' My momma asked.

"That's that bitch daughter," I spat and made my way out the hospital.

My momma doesn't know, but Ace and I went to see the baby before she got here. And when I looked at her, I knew that she was mine because she looked just like our son. I don't have shit to say to Bri, and I don't think I ever will. I called the lawyer because we were going to court. They can make all the decisions and mediate because I don't even want to be in that bitch presence again if I don't have to.

"You good?" Ace asked as we stepped on the elevator.

"Naw, but I will be."

Ace and I shook up once we got off the elevator and went our separate ways. He had to go and check on Mina and he been up here all day with me. I jumped in my car and headed to OG's to get Tamera. My phone started ringing and it was OG.

"What's wrong?" I asked as my phone connected to my car's Bluetooth.

"Tamera is upset. Something about her friend Darius is leaving and going back to Arizona. She's been crying since I picked her up. Do you know what's going on with Modesty? I thought she just got her son back," OG replied.

"I'm going to go and check on them, and then I'll be there," I assured her and changed lanes to go and see what the fuck is going on like I got a fucking cape on.

Tamera hated that school until she started hanging around Lil D. I can't have her upset, crying and shit. Then I'll have to fight with her every morning to go to school again. Luckily, that place I seen her coming out of ain't that far from here.

"Bitch go! I don't have all fucking day! Better yet, take yo' ass back to Illinoi's!" I screamed out the window at this dumb bitch in traffic.

It took me about twenty minutes and I finally made it. As I pulled up to the house I seen Chocolate coming out of the other day, she was in front of the house arguing with somebody. Why the fuck is she even here? These places are for people that are in need and getting beat on. Modesty is a lot of shit, but in need ain't one of 'em.

"Come on," I said, pulling Modesty away from the woman.

"Why the fuck are you here?" Modesty questioned, snatching away from me.

"A better question is why the fuck are you here? Give me yo' keys," I said. She wasn't moving at all so I snatched them then went to her car and got Lil' D out the backseat.

"He not going nowhere with you. Either come with me or I'm gon' call Gotti. Them are yo' fucking choices," I said, getting Lil D into my car.

She hesitated, but she started getting her bags out of her truck. I popped my trunk as I got back into the car. I'm not helping her ungrateful ass. She got in my car and slammed my door. I rubbed my hands over my face trying to calm down because I ain't ever hit a bitch. But these bitches is real close to getting hit.

"Get the fuck out my car, get back in and close my door the right fucking way," I said as calmly as I could for Lil D's sake.

"What?" Modesty questioned.

I looked at her, and she got her ass out the car and did what I told her to do. I have to keep remembering that this is for Tamera. Modesty hasn't said anything and I gave Lil D Tamera's tablet that she left in the car. I made my way to my old house because she ain't coming to my damn new house. Ain't nobody staying there, so she can stay there for a fucking limited time.

"Huh, Lil mans, go on head and go in. You can take that with you," I said, handing him the key to the house, and he didn't ask no questions. He said bye then jumped out my car and ran up to the house.

"You ain't got to tell me what the fuck is going on with you. To be honest, I don't really give a fuck. I'm here because my daughter came home crying about yo' son having to move back with his dad. Get yo' shit together because I ain't in the business of taking care of bitches and I very rarely let them spend the night," I said, looking over at Modesty.

"Thanks," she mumbled.

"Don't thank me, get yo' shit together for yo' son," I said, unlocking the doors because they locked when I put the car in drive.

EPILOGUE

Ahmina

"I'm glad you got yo' self together," Kurupt said as he walked in the house and Kai playfully hit him.

"He's rude as hell, he ain't got no home training," I said, laughing as I stood up to go and hug him.

It seems like he's been gone forever, but it has only been four months. Even with them not having a case without Tycoon, they tried all types of shit to keep him, but it didn't work. Today is a big day. Not only did K come home today, but it's the grand opening of me and Mo's boutique. Mo didn't want Gotti or any of our family involved in the finance part of our business, so she came up with her half. I had mine from the money that I had from Tycoon's family and we made it happen.

"Will you go get dressed, so you're on time?" I said as K sat down, getting comfortable.

"What the fuck do I have to be on time for? It ain't mine. You wouldn't even let me help yo' ass," K spat, turning on the TV.

"You help me with everything. What happened to you letting me figure shit out on my own and being an adult."

"Fuck all that," K said, and Kai looked at him crazy. "I'm just playing."

"Come help me get dressed before I have to beat up Mina," K said, getting up and wrapping his arms around Kai as she led the way out the room.

"Come on, they can get there without yo' help," Ace said as he stood in the doorway just staring at me holding Tiana's big ass.

It hasn't been an easy ride this past few months and for a minute there, I didn't think that we were going to make it, but we did. I still have days where I want to kill him and Big Face, but at the end of the day, this is where I want to be, so I have to put in the work to make it work. Today is also Mo's birthday. She had a party last night, so she better have her ass here on time. I been talking to her all day on and off. She told me she would be there but knowing her, who knows when she'll be there.

"Everything is going to be good, relax," Ace said as he opened my door for me to get in the car that is driving us.

He be cussing out the driver every time he tries to do his dam job. After the first two times, I had to just tell the man just drive and nothing else. But, I guess it's a habit, so he always goes to get out of the car then remembers and gets back in. Ace has changed a lot and he made accommodations for me and Tiana without me even asking. Since that night, he came back to the house and Tycoon was there when he came back, he hasn't left my house. And when he does, he comes back every night. He calls me to make sure that I'm good throughout the day and he's there for Tiana whenever I need him. He's definitely putting in work at home and in the streets. The position that he has with the family has been paying off for him and Big Face.

"Everything is going to be just how you want it to be, relax and enjoy it. You been bustin' yo' ass to get this shit right. I got you, I love you, Ahmina," Ace assured me.

"Okay, I love you too," I said.

That is the first time that we've ever said that too each other and even though I agreed with him, I can't help but to be nervous. This was never something that I wanted, but I know how bad Mo wanted it. She hasn't had it easy lately, and I wanted to support her in any way that I could.

When we pulled up and I saw Mo's truck, I was surprised that she was early. Her ass is always running late. Ace got out the car with Tiana clinging on to him and came over to open my door. He kissed me on the cheek, then on my forehead and grabbed my hand. I don't know why I'm so damn nervous, but I am. When I walked in and Mo screamed my name, it helped me calm down a little.

I can't get the letter that I got in the mail from Lady H out of my mind. I hadn't seen or heard from her since she left my house, but that letter just opened some wounds that I thought I was over. When I got the DNA results back saying that Sharonda was my mom, I didn't know how to feel. I haven't seen her or talked to her and don't plan to. She got what she wanted; Shakim is in. Kurupt has him working with Big Face and Ace. Ace likes him, but Big Face treats the nigga like his fucking servant. I guess he has to pay his dues and if he ain't complaining, I can't say nothing about it either.

"Why the fuck is he here? Did you invite him?" Mo asked as I turned around and saw Big Face.

"No, I didn't invite him, but you act like you mad. You still be talking to him. You live in the niggas house. Y'all need to quit playing and just fuck with each other."

"Fuck him, he didn't even come to my birthday party last night. I didn't even get a happy birthday from him," Mo whined.

"That's why you mad. That nigga done offered for you to go

places and all types of shit, and you always turn him down. Why would he come to yo' birthday party?" I asked, and she rolled her eyes.

"Who the fuck invited you?" Mo asked as Big Face walked over to where we were standing behind the cash register.

Big Face has roses in his hand and when he handed them to me, I was confused and Mo was mad as hell. This nigga was smiling so damn hard and that was pissing her off. The way he is looking at her, I feel like we need to let them talk. By the mean bitch face that Mo has on, I know that I should probably just stay over here to keep her calm.

"I came to get my rent money. I don't know who you thought you were paying with a fucking check, but I accept cash only and you already know that."

"Fuck you, Big Face," Mo spat and walked away.

"Why you didn't you come to the party las night? And why haven't you told her happy birthday?" I asked. Ace cleared his throat and looked at me crazy.

"Her birthday ain't over, and I ain't going to a bitch birthday party that won't give me no pussy like she ain't gave it to half the fucking city. Now she trying to find herself and lighting sage every other day like she's a new person. Fuck that and her."

"Mina, mind yo' own damn business," Ace suggested.

"Hey, Ahmina, it's time to cut the ribbon," Yari, our party planner, said as she walked over to us.

We all made our way outside, so we could open up the boutique to the public. I let Mo handle all of the merchandise. I didn't have anything to do with that. She did a good job and everything looks really nice. As Mo talked, I looked over and Gotti was coming over with Lil D. When Mo saw Lil D and he saw her, he took off running to be by her side. I'm so glad that she didn't call Darius and send Lil D back to Arizona. Having him full-time made her grow up and be more responsible. The fact that she did everything without Gotti's help means the most to her. Gotti wasn't too happy when he found out what she was going through then not telling him or letting him help, but he got over it. Even with all that Mo has been though with her mom, she invited her. I could tell as Mo scanned the crowd she was looking for her, but she wasn't out here.

"Mina, come over here!" Mo yelled.

I made my way over to her and on the count of three, me, her and Lil D cut the ribbon on the door to our new adventure. Big Face popped a bottle like he was involved in any way. A car pulled up and Kai and Kurupt's late ass got out. I'm just glad that they are here.

"Where is OG?" I whispered to Ace.

"There she is over there with Lu and Tamera," Ace said, pointing over to them playing the back.

I made my way over to them to speak. I didn't ask about Joy because I didn't invite her, and I damn sure don't care if she comes or not. She has tried to talk to me since Ace and I have been back together, but I'm not interested in talking to her about nothing. OG is still so sweet and she's doing really good. Her cancer is still in remission and since her and Lu have been back together, she seems to be happier than I have ever seen her. Ace and Lu aren't best friends, but they are at least talking, so I'm not complaining. I felt somebody tap me on my shoulder and it was Joy holding Big Face's daughter, Simone.

"Look, I know we don't fuck with each other like that and I ain't trying to be yo 'friend or nothing, but I wanted to say congratulations," Joy said and half-smiled.

"Thank you," I said as I turned around because Ace was screaming my name on a microphone.

Mo rushed over to me and started ushering me closer to him. Looking around, everybody was smiling and pulling out their phones. Mo was just too damn happy. What the fuck is going on? Ace isn't even the type of nigga to talk that much, let a lone in front of all these people.

"Mina, we've been through some shit, but I wouldn't trade any of it because I know that if we made it through that, we can make it through anything. We still got some work to do, but I'm ready to do it. I don't want nobody else and nobody else better want you. You and Tiana are already mine, but I want to make it official," Ace said as he dropped down on one knee.

Mo and Kurupt pushed me like I was taking too long to get over to him.

"I need somebody else to take care yo ass, get to moving," Kurupt whispered into my ear.

Ace threw the mic down and looked up at me.

"Will you marry me?" Ace asked as Tiana grabbed onto my leg.

"Yes," I said, shaking my head up and down as tears of joy ran down my face.

BIG FACE

"Why the hell did you bring Mina flowers?" Ace asked me.

"Nigga, I don't want Mina. I bought them for Chocolate, but she still on her bullshit," I admitted.

"Nigga, since when you start buying bitches flowers?"

"Fuck you," I said as my momma walked over to where Ace and I were standing.

"Are you with Mo yet?" My momma asked.

"No," I said, taking my daughter from her arms.

This has taken some getting used to; not only having one daughter but having two is some shit that I never seen for a nigga. The mediator worked shit out with Bri and I. My momma is the mediator, and she does all the communicating to Bri. She's tried to talk to me on several occasions, but I don't have shit to say to her. I just let my momma deal with her.

"I don't know why. You just gon' be old and alone," my momma said.

"Yea, just like my momma," I said. She didn't like that shit but since Mo don't even like her, she didn't get crazy.

She took Simone from me and walked away. I looked around for Mo and she was walking around greeting and helping customers. When she got that job that she hated, she didn't last long. But when she got fired, she went back to her old business. She did it long enough to hustle up the money to start this boutique. I didn't ask her for rent money that was her idea and all the money that she has given me over the past three months, I put in an account for her son. I don't need it, and she's still trying to get on her feet.

"Why don't you just talk to her? I need her to be occupied, so she can stay out of my damn business," Ace requested.

"She want that shit that you and Mina got, and that ain't what I'm offering," I said as I took my bottle of Bellaire to the head.

"Why? You done cut off all the bitches you was fucking with."

"I don't have time for 'em."

I walked away from Ace and walked over to Chocolate now that she wasn't talking to anybody. She looked good as hell and for once, she got some fucking clothes on. I'm surprised because that ain't her style.

"This shit turned out nice. You did a good job," I admitted, looking around.

"Not today, I don't want to hear none of yo' bullshit. First you don't show up to my birthday party then you show up and bring Mina flowers on my birthday. Your an asshole!" Mo said like she didn't hear what the fuck I said.

"Shut the fuck up," I said as I got closer to her and wrapped my arms around her. I bit her lip and then kissed her like I've been wanting too for a minute now.

At first, she put up a fight and had a nigga looking strange as hell, but after a few seconds of me gripping on her ass, she gave in and kissed me back. I don't know what the fuck is going to happen with us, but I know she got to work on her fucking attitude and getting her shit together. She got me doing shit that I don't do and no matter what, I can't get her off my fucking mind. Everybody was bringing her up, from my bitches to my family.

"Big Face, I'm not about to play with you," Chocolate said as she broke our kiss and I still held on to her.

"Shut up, damn you ruin everything," I said.

"I'm not playing and that shit that them bitches be allowing, I'm not dealing with that shit," Chocolate said, giving me an ultimatum.

"Alright, you can be my Monday th—" I attempted to say before I was cut off.

"You got me fucked up, get the fuck off me!" Chocolate yelled, trying to snatch away.

"If you'd shut the fuck up, so I can talk. I was trying to say my Monday through Sunday," I said, laughing because she was mad as hell.

"Finally! My mom really like you, she be talking about—" Lil D attempted to say as he came running towards us, but Chocolate put her hand over his mouth.

Chocolate gave him a look and he ran off as my momma brought her nosy ass over to where we were. I know that she was embarrassed, but I know that she wanted a nigga, but been playing like she didn't. I know that I said that I would never fuck with her like that, but the bitch that I thought eventually I would end up with turned out to be a snake. I had to let that go and move on. Even though Choc ain't at her best right now, I know that she can get there with some help and guidance whether she wants it or not.

"Um, what the fuck y'all doing?" My momma asked.

"'Bout to go in one of these dressing rooms," I said, looking around for the dressing rooms.

"Shut up, no, we not," Choc said, hugging me tight.

"Don't make no more fucking kids," my momma said, hitting me and walked away.

"Hey bitch, give me that shit that you just stuffed in yo'

purse!" I yelled to this bitch that was in here trying to hit a lick. I let go of Choc and went over to the bitch.

"Excuse me," the bitch said. I let Mo go then went over to her and emptied her Victoria Secret duffle bag onto the floor.

"I'm gon' need to be paid for my services if I got be security in this bitch!" I said as Mina, Mo and Yari rushed over to us.

THE END

SNEAK PEAK OF WHAT'S NEXT...

PROLOGUE

2009

TATIANA

"Yes, momma I went to school today," I lied as I washed the dishes and heard Jamir started to whine.

"Then what is this Tatii? I hate a lying ass bitch," My momma said as she played the recording that said her student in twelfth grade missed one or more classes today.

"That's wrong, I was a late to my first class because Amir was late picking up Jamir," I said but she wasn't trying to hear that.

My momma can't stand Amir and this is just another reason for her to start talking her shit. Just like clockwork she started talking shit. This was nothing new because my family always has something to say about him. Except my nigga auntie Boo. I don't care because tomorrow when I tun eighteen I'm getting the fuck out of her and her husband's house, so whatever I do will be my business and she can keep her opinions on Maple street because I won't be here to listen to them.

"Tatiana when are you going to see that nigga doesn't give a fuck about you. Soon, you will have two kids that you need to be worried about. All you want to do is run behind that nigga. When is the last time that you took yo ass to work? What are you going to do when his ass is on Cooper street because you and Jamir won't be in matching Jordan's then? That nigga ain't bought shit for your daughter and she'll be here before you know it," My momma nagged.

I didn't say anything because I'll end up arguing with her about Amir and I'm not about to do that with her today. I finished washing the dishes and went to go and get Jamir. Amir has bought everything that Jalayna will need and it's set up at his house in her room. I know that my mom is not going to be happy when after I leave here today, I never come back, but I can't do this no more. She wants Amir to step up and do more and that is exactly what he is doing.

When I went to get Jamir, my dad had him and was tossing him up in the air. Me and my dad were close when I was younger, but when I got with Amir all that change. You would think my dad was a saint that went to church every Sunday, but that is far from his past. My momma stuck it out with him, so I don't understand why they have such a problem with Amir. Unlike my mom my dad Bryce just barely says anything to me. He talks his shit to my mom and she damn sure delivers it to me, but he just barely talks to me and that works for us.

"Hey Pops!" D'Sharii said as she came in the front door.

"What's going on daughter?" My dad said getting up and hugging D.

He kills me, he doesn't like the way that I'm living my life, but D'Sharii is a perfect princess in his eyes. Even though her nigga is in the streets just like Amir, but he acts like that's not the case. My momma on the other hand can't stand D'Sharii and she doesn't mind telling her every time she sees her. I don't know what her issue is with D'Sharii but I'm sure it's some of her good bullshit.

"Alright, it's time for yo lil' friend to go and you need to be back in this house before the clock strikes twelve or that key won't work," My momma said as she came into the living room talking with her hands.

I made my way to the kitchen to get my phone off the charger and my pop out of the refrigerator. I had taken almost all of me and Jamir's clothes out the house and everything else we already have one at Amir's. I'm not worried because I know that Amir has me and Jamir just like he always has from day one and my parents will get over it one day and if they don't o' well. I snatched up Jamir's car seat and darted for the door.

"Did you hear what I said Tatiana?" My momma asked as I grabbed the door handle.

"Yes, I heard you," I said and D'Sharii followed me out the door carrying Jamir.

"Yo' momma get on my nerves just as much as my own damn momma. I ain't never did nothing to her old ass."

"Girl we don't have to worry about her because I'm not coming back here," I admitted.

"So, you serious about moving with Amir?" D'Sharii questioned.

"Yup," I said as we got into D'Sharii's car.

As D started up the car, "You Complete me," by Keyshia Cole, came through the speakers. D'Sharii is my best friend and has been since fifth grade. I couldn't stand her ass for years and we fought like cats and dogs. After our last fight our Principle Mr. Cook made us have a meeting with our parents and My momma and her dad was sick of our shit, so they made us be cool. I was still picking and being mean for another week, but when I saw this other girl that I couldn't stand. This white girl named Ashley Smith fucking with her I beat her ass instead that day and we been cool ever since.

D'Sharii doesn't really care for Amir, but she doesn't like nobody but Drama's ass. If it ain't about Drama she doesn't care about it. Even though she doesn't agree with my decision to be with Amir it has never came in between our friendship.

"When are you gon' bring yo ass to work? If you keep calling in, they gon' fire yo ass," D'Sharii nagged.

"I don't give a fuck about that job. I hate that fucking place. Them people get on my damn nerves. I got all the credits that I need for co-op to graduate, so they can fire me for all the fuck I care."

"What you gon' do? Because yet Lil' Kim, Biggie ain't made yo dreams come true. And you need to be getting yo own bag."

I didn't even say nothin' back to D'Sharii, I looked back at Jamir and he's knocked out in the backseat. I know that she's just being a real friend but this shit isn't easy. Taking care of Jamir going to school enough to keep my grades up, so I can graduate in a few weeks. Then trying to work at Ganton Retirement Center, not for the money but so I can get credit for school, is so much. I've been, so tired that I fall asleep in the shower some nights.

"You want some Coney Island?" D'Sharii asked.

"Yea," I said thinking about the fact that I'll probably be in the house alone with Jamir.

"And bitch, I want Jackson not Virginia because I know how yo ass is."

I rolled my eyes knowing that I am going to have to carry Jamir's big ass down the block to Virginia because Jackson been fuckin' up lately and I want my shit right. I never imagined this life for myself but my decisions got me here. Don't get me wrong I love Jamir and Jalayna, but I didn't plan on having them right now. Jamir is only two and I'm due any day now. I'm the only bitch that I know on birth control and still get pregnant not once, but twice. I even switched from the pill to depo and I still ended up pregnant.

We made it to Coney Island and D'Sharii looked at me, rolling her eyes and got out the car and made her way to

Virginia already knowing my regular order. She gon' be talking shit when she gets back in the car, but I don't care as long as she gets my food and the right way. D'Sharii flicked me off as she made her way down the street to Jackson Coney Island to order her food.

"Don't forget my chocolate malt from there!" I yelled out the car and she flicked me off with two fingers.

My phone started ringing and it's Kamarii my only other friend other than D'Sharii. I might associate with a few other bitches, but them bitches ain't my bitches.

"Hello," I said as I answered.

"Biiiiiiittttchhhhh! Ain't you with D?" Kamarii asked.

"Yea, what is going on now? Mouth of the south," I asked because I know the way she just sang in my ear it's some bullshit.

"Where's D, so I can tell y'all together?" Kamarii asked as my phone started beeping, but it's my momma so I didn't answer it.

I caught Marii up on what was going on with me. And she told me her and Keyontae drama. It's always something with them and to be honest, like I always tell her ass it's her because she stays on bullshit. She hangs around her brother and his friends, so much that she thinks she's a nigga. I see why Keyontae stay on her ass because she always on some hoe shit.

As she tells me about, their latest fight, I can't help but to shake my head because out of all three of us, her ass is the only one that want to hop around to different niggas. Her issue is that Keyontae isn't in the streets and getting fast money. Keyontae is a regular guy he goes to school and works at KFC. That's not good enough for her, you would think the bitch was raised in a house on a hill and not on the corner of South Jackson and Biddle.

"Bitch, this shit ain't easy and you need to work shit out

with Keyontae because none of them other niggas give a fuck about you," I admitted.

"What that hoe done did now? D asked as she got in the car shaking her head, handing me my food and malt.

"Bittttchhh! From what I just heard while I was getting my nails done. You got some shit that you need to be worried about," Marii said and she is on speaker, so D heard her.

As Kamarii ran down what she heard about Drama, D started crying her eyes out. We haven't even left Coney Island yet. It's always some bullshit when it comes to Drama but D'Sharii keeps holding on to the hope that he will change. She is stronger than I could ever be because if Amir tried any of the shit that Drama pulls, I wouldn't be able to stay with him no matter how much I love him.

D wiped away her tears and Keyshia Cole blared through the car, as she started it up. Looking back at Jamir he is still sleep. If he can sleep through my momma and dad arguing about me and their shit then he can sleep through anything. But when we get in the house he is about to get woke up because he is not about to be up all night. I ended my call with Marii and D hasn't said anything yet. When she gets quiet is when I worry because I know that she wants to tear up some shit, but I am in no condition to jump out on Drama.

"D, you want to talk about it?" I asked as D turned at the light.

"For what? This nigga is never going to change. I'm, so sick of this shit Tatii. Here I am holding him down, going to school, working and he's out here all in these hoes faces. Deja this week and who the fuck is it going to be next week?" D said as tears started to well up in her eyes again.

"You can do better D. Look at you. Your taking classes at Michigan State University, with straight A's there and at the high and getting closer to your dream. You killed that shit with Jamir's birthday party. You put in work for my baby shower. You don't need Drama. I know that you love him, but is it worth the headache?"

"I'm tired Tatii," D said throwing the car in park as we pulled up to the house.

"I know my baby," I said as D started balling her eyes out and I got out of my seatbelt to hug her.

Amir came outside and when he seen D crying, he shook his head and mouthed he loved me and came and got Jamir out of the car. Amir talks his shit, but he tells D all the time to leave Drama. He even has tried to hook her up with several niggas that wanted to talk to her. She shot them all down. Amir supplies Drama but it's business and nothing more. He won't hang with Drama or his crew. If it's not about some money they have nothin to talk about. I have told Amir to stop fuckin' with Drama but he always says the same thing.

I held D as she cried into my shoulder like I do whenever she needs a shoulder to lean on. Through everything we have always been there for each other, so if she stays with Drama or leaves, I'll be here and I'm not going anywhere. We have been through so much shit and it has been many of days and we were the only ones there for each other. Kamarii is there when she can be, but she been on so much bullshit lately she hardly ever has time.

D is beautiful, caramel with a lot of honey complexion. D's skin is, so clear I never seen her with a pimple. She has long curly black hair that she got from her momma because her daddies' people are damn near all bald headed. And her daddy's deep brown eyes. D has the perfect shape, hardly not any titties and a donk. Lately she hardly ever smiles and is always walking around muggin' every damn body.

"I love him Tatii but I don't want to end up like Martha," D cried out.

"I know but you have to love yourself D. Fuck Drama, he ain't shit and if he doesn't know what he has then you need to be what he had," I said as I got her some napkins out of the glove compartment.

D wiped her nose and pulled out a blunt and hit it hard. I've tried to smoke, but it just wasn't for me. I be moving too damn slow to do anything. D on the other hand is a weed head. I can drink, but D can do both with no problem. She can be high and go and kill a test and go to work like it ain't shit. I fanned away her weed smoke that is invading my nostrils and D laughed and rolled down all the windows.

"You want to come in?" I asked.

Before I could finish my question good, Jasmine Sullivan, "Need you bad," came from D's phone and I knew what that meant even though she sent him to the voicemail. She's about to go to take granny her car and Drama is going to come and pick her up. I don't want that for her, but she is going to do what she is going to do. Just like I figured, she told me she had to take granny back her car.

"Call me when you get to grannie's, bitch!" I said in between biting into one of my Coney's and trying to hand D her money.

"Alright, bitch bye. Put that money in Jamir's piggy bank and you better have yo ass at work tomorrow unless you go into labor," D said and took more pulls from her blunt.

Rolling my eyes, I got out the car and made my way into the house and a beat that Amir is trying to convince me to rap on this track blared throughout the house. I know this is just another attempt to get me on the track with his homie. I don't know, why but I'm just not feeling it. No matter how Amir tries to persuade me to get on the track and how it could help get some buzz. For my mixtape, that I plan on dropping the day that I have Jalayna. Once I have Jalayna I can perform and make videos. I have some tracks out now, but I'm only buzzing locally.

"Do you know what this track could do for you? I'm telling you this is the one," Amir yelled over the beat.

"Okay, I'll do it," I said flopping down on the couch.

I ate my food as I wrote the course and my verse in my head. Amir sat down next to me and took off my sandals that were killing my swollen feet and rubbed them. We aren't talking because Amir knows me and he knows that I need silence to create. The beat stopped and Amir grabbed the remote to the DVD player and played it again.

"What are you doing tonight?" I asked knowing the answer.

"I have to make some moves, and I'll be back home," Amir replied.

"Whatever."

"I know that it's a lot going on but I got us and you already know that. Whatever you and the kids need, I'm gon' make sure that y'all get it. To make that happen right now, I have to make these moves."

As Amir took me into his arms. I feel safe, loved and I know that he feels the same way about me. Amir is twenty and that plays a big part in my family's disapproval, but I don't care. Because no matter what anybody says I'm going to always love Amir. He is everything that any girl could ever want. He's a provider, patient, protector and proud.

"I love you, Tatii," Amir said as he hugged me a caressed my stomach.

"I love you too baby."

When Amir's phone rang, I knew what that meant even though he hasn't moved yet. It's either Dough or some money on the floor and either way he's about to leave. As he started kissing me all over my face, I knew that he was about to leave. We laid on the couch for about thirty more minutes. Amir begged to hear my verse and the hook and I finally gave in. Amir jumped off the couch and hyped me up like only he can do and started playing the beat again.

"This is it," Amir said as he bopped his head and lit a blunt as I sang the hook.

I couldn't help but smile because whenever I'm around Amir he makes me smile. He makes me better. In this world I have, so many people counting me out and there is Amir riding with me through it all. The ups and the down's he's never switched up. His momma and sister can't stand me for no reason but any time the ever tried to come at me sideways Amir won't hesitate to put them in their place. I went into Jamir's room to check on him and he's playing with his tablet with his TV blasting.

"Pick one Mir," I said and he got up and turned off the TV.

Amir came into the room and picked up Mir and threw him in the air. The bond that they have I never want that to change. Little boys need their father and I pray that no matter what the bond they have will never be broken. Amir put Mir down and slapped me on my ass as I picked up some toys off the floor.

"Stop, that hurts," I whined and Amir took me into his arms and smacked my ass again.

"Shut up, this is mine all mine and I can touch it whenever and however I want too," Amir spat and started kissing me all over.

"Bye Amir and I don't give a fuck how much money is on the floor you better not let the sun beat you home," I said meaning every word because I know Amir's black ass.

Amir is dark chocolate, chubby and even though he hovers me he isn't that tall. He's flashy, is always wearing all this damn jewelry and no matter how much I complain about it and him being a walking lick he still puts all of it on every morning after he puts his heat on his waist. He has pretty, perfect teeth and dimples big enough for me to jump in. He's the type of nigga that every bitch wants and if they know what's best for them and Amir, they better always stay arm's length.

"Soon, as I get home," Amir attempted to sing.

He sounds so bad that Jamir covered his ears. We both busted out laughing because we all know that he sounds a hot mess. I led the way to the door because if Amir doesn't leave now or misses out on some bread, I'll hear about it for the next month. Amir kissed me and caressed my stomach as we walked to the door and Jalayna started going crazy kicking the shit out of me. My phone started ringing and by the ringtone Swagga like us, by "T.I," blared through my Nextel, I know that it's D'Sharii.

∾

"AMIR," I said as I rolled over looking at the time on the alarm clock on the nightstand and it's almost 2 am.

I heard the front door open and it has to be Amir down there making all that noise. I rolled out of bed and peeked my head into Jamir's room to check on him and he's still asleep. He can sleep through anything. S, I made my way downstairs.

What the fuck is Amir doing down there?

"Amir, really it's 2 in the mornin' and your down here making all this damn noise! And why don't you have the light on?" I asked turning on the light.

When I turned on the light as I made my way through the downstairs, I can't believe my eyes. Everything is destroyed from the tv to Jamir's playpen. Everything is flipped over and I doubt I'll be able to save anything with stench of gasoline that just hit my nose hard. I took off running for the stairs once I seen two niggas in masks in the kitchen. While praying the whole time that they didn't hear me.

"Bitch, where's the dope at?" One of the two masked men asked before my foot could hit the first step.

"It's not none..." I attempted to say before one of the men hit me in the back of my head with his gun and I clung onto the rail on the stairs to stop myself from falling.

While trying to hold on to the rail and grippin' my stomach with the other one tears started to fall down my face. All I want to do is make sure that Jamir gets out of here and that my daughter isn't hurt as well. I don't know where Amir keeps his dope at, its never been a reason for me to know until now.

"Where the fuck the money at?" One of them asked.

Pop! Pop! Pop!

Bullets started flying through the windows and one by one they were going so fast and ruining everything that these other niggas hadn't. The nigga in the house or the ones outside are going to have to kill me because I'm going to get my baby. I struggled to make my way upstairs while praying to God to keep us safe.

I got in Jamir's room and picked him up and brought him to mine and Amir's room and ran into the closet locking the door behind us. I can still here all the commotion downstairs, but there is no way that I can make it out the house alive walking back downstairs, so I weighed my options. While Jamir screamed, so loud that I don't know if the gun play going on downstairs or Jamir was louder.

After about five minutes all of the shooting stopped and it got uncomfortably quiet as I tried to get Jamir to stop crying. I can hear somebody running up the stairs.

"Somebody is in this bitch and I'm not leaving empty handed, so look muthafucka!" Someone yelled while I sat on the floor rocking Jamir as he finally stopped screaming.

When I heard them getting closer and closer my heart started beating so fast that I thought it was going to jump out of my chest.

Boom! The sound of the bedroom door being kicked in, had my stomach tight and caused Jamir to stir as I rocked and prayed silently to let us make it out of here alive.

Boom! Next thing I knew the closet door was being kicked down and I was starring at four new niggas and they all looked like they didn't have shit to lose.

"Where's the money at?" One of them asked

"I..." I attempted to say before one of them men snatched me up and another pried Jamir out of my arms.

Next thing I knew a gun was pressed to my right ear and cocked back.

Pop!

Coming In OCTOBER...